AFTER BREAD

AFTER BREAD

A Story of Polish Emigrant Life to America

BY THE AUTHOR OF

"QUO VADIS"

(HENRYK SIENKIEWICZ)

Translated from the Polish by

VATSLAF A. HLASKO AND THOMAS H. BULLICK

Fredonia Books
Amsterdam, The Netherlands

After Bread:
A Story of Polish Emigrant Life to America

by
Henryk Sienkiewicz

ISBN: 1-58963-529-9

Reprinted from the 1897 edition

Fredonia Books
Amsterdam, The Netherlands
http://www.fredoniabooks.com

In order to make original editions of historical works available to scholars at an economical price, this facsimile of the original edition of 1897 is reproduced from the best available copy and has been digitally enhanced to improve legibility, but the text remains unaltered to retain historical authenticity.

AFTER BREAD.

CHAPTER I.

ON the waves of the wide ocean rode
the German steamer Blucher, on its passage from Hamburg to New York.

It had been on its way four days. Two
days ago it had passed the green coast of
Ireland and reached the broad Atlantic.
From the deck, as far as the eye could
reach, could be seen the gray and green
surface, plowed up in furrows and hol-
lows, rocking heavily, foaming in places,
in the distance more dark, where the
water joined the sky in a white, cloudy
mist.

The reflection from the clouds fell some-times upon the water, and upon this pearly background was drawn with sharp outlines the figure of the steamer. The ship, with its bow pointing to the west, climbed to the crest of the billows, and then, as if going to drown itself, sank in the trough of the sea; sometimes it disappeared from view, sometimes it was lifted so high on the top of the waves that part of its keel could be seen—still pressed steadily onward. The waves rolled toward it, and it rushed toward the waves and cut them with its prow. Behind it chased, like a gigantic snake, a wide strip of foaming water; several sea-gulls followed in its wake, circling in the air with their wild cries.

The wind was fresh; and the vessel pro-ceeded under half-steam with all its sails set. The weather promised to become finer. In places, between the broken clouds, could be seen patches of blue, constantly changing form. Since the Blucher had left the port of Hamburg it had encountered strong winds, but no storms. The winds were westerly, but at times they ceased; then the sails flapped and fluttered, to be shortly filled out like the breast of the swan. The sailors, in their blue woolen sweaters, dragged the rope of the lower yard, as they monotonously cried " Yo-hoy! yo-hoy!" bending and straightening themselves, keeping time with the song; and their cries mingled with the boatswain's whistle and the puffing of the funnel.

To enjoy the fine weather the passengers had come out on the deck. In the stern of the ship could be observed the black overcoats and hats of the cabin passengers; in the forward part was a motley crowd of emigrants from the steerage. Some of them sat on benches, smoking short pipes, some

were lying down, others were leaning against
the rail, looking into the water.

There were several women with children
in their arms and tin platters fastened to
their belts; several young men promenaded
from the bow to the bridge, trying to keep
their equilibrium with poor success.
They sang " *Wo ist das deutsche Vaterland!*" and, perhaps, they thought that
they would never see their "*Vaterland*"
again; but, notwithstanding this, they did
not seem downcast.

Among this crowd were two who were
most sad and who kept apart from the
others: an old man and a maiden. They
did not understand German and felt very
lonely among strangers. They were Polish
peasants.

The man's name was Lorenz Toporek,
and the girl, Mary, was his daughter.
They were coming to America, and had
just now, for the first time, plucked up

courage to venture upon deck. Upon
their faces, pale from seasickness, was
painted fear, mingled with curiosity.
With timid eyes they looked upon their
fellow-passengers, the sailors, the ship,
the huge smokestack, puffing violently,
the formidable waves, throwing spray on
the deck, and they dared not speak. With
one hand Lorenz held the rail, and with
the other he held on his head his odd-
fashioned four-cornered cap, so that the
wind would not blow it off; and Mary
stood close by her father, and as often as
the ship lurched from side to side she
grasped him, exclaiming faintly from
fear. Shortly the old man broke the
silence:

" Mary."

" What is it, father?"

" Do you see?"

" I do."

" Do you marvel?"

"I do indeed."

Still she feared more than she wondered, and so did old Toporek. Fortunately for them the waves subsided, the wind ceased and the sun broke through the clouds. When they saw the "beloved sun" they felt more easy in their hearts, for it looked to them exactly as it did in Lipintse. All to them was new and strange, and only this disk of the sun, bright and radiant, appeared like an old friend and guardian.

The sea became smoother; soon the sails slackened; from the bridge sounded the signal whistle of the captain, and the sailors rushed to furl them. The sight of the men, apparently hanging in the air above the abyss, again astonished Toporek and Mary.

"Our boys could not do that," said the old man.

"If the Dutchmen can climb, John could climb also," said Mary.

"Which John—Sobkow?"

"Why Sobkow? I mean Smolak, the hostler."

"He is very dexterous, but you must put him out of your head; you are coming to America to be a lady, while he will remain, as he is, a hostler."

"He has some property."

"If he has, it is in Lipintse."

Mary did not answer, but only thought that fate could not be avoided. She sighed deeply, and meanwhile the sails were furled, and, instead, the screw began to churn the water, so that the whole vessel trembled and its rocking motion ceased. In the far distance the water appeared smooth and blue. More people appeared on the deck: artisans, German peasants, idlers from different seaports, who were coming to America to seek pleasure—not

work; the deck was so crowded that Lorenz
and Mary sought a secluded spot and sat
on a coil of rope in a corner near the bow.

"Father, how much longer shall we be
on the sea?" inquired Mary.

"How do I know? those whom you ask
answer you as a heathen."

"How shall we speak in America?"

"Did they not say that there was a
multitude of our own people there?"

"Father?"

"What is it?"

"Talk as you may, I feel that it was
better in Lipintse."

Lorenz Toporek pondered. Why was
he going to America, and how did it happen? Six months ago, last summer, his
cow broke into a neighbor's clover, and
they seized and took it to the pound. The
farmer who did this wanted three rubles
damages; Lorenz did not want to pay.
They went to law; the suit was prolonged;

the farmer not only wanted damages, but also costs for the cow's keep, and the costs grew every day. Lorenz was obstinate, thought this was unfair, and did not wish to part with his money. He spent a large amount on the lawsuit, and it dragged and dragged. The costs constantly grew larger, and at last Lorenz was defeated. He owed for his cow a large amount, and because he now had no money to pay it, they took his horse and arrested him for resisting the officer. Toporek struggled to get out of his difficulty. It needed both his horse and his own labor to harvest his crop. He was late in housing his grain; the rains fell and it sprouted in the sheaves, and he saw that, for the small damage of his cow, his crops were ruined, his property was scattered, and for the coming winter starvation stared them in the face.

Having been previously a fairly well-to-

do farmer, he became despondent and
began to drink. At the inn he met
a German, who pretended to be a flax-
buyer, but who was in reality an emigrant steamship agent. This German ex-
patiated on the wonders and marvels of
America. He promised him for nothing
more land than the largest farm in Lipintse—together with woods and pasture
lands, so that the peasant's eyes beamed
with anticipation. He believed, yet
doubted, but the Jew milk-merchant, who
accompanied the German, said that the
American government gave to everybody
as much land as they could use. The Jew
had been so informed by his nephew.
The German exhibited a larger roll of
money than the peasant, or even the landlord, had ever seen before. They tempted
the peasant till they secured him. Why
should he remain here? But for the damages that he had sustained through his cow

he could have kept a helper. Will he go to
rack and ruin? Will he take a staff in his
hand and sing, like the beggars under the
church, "Holy heavenly Lady, angelic,
praise be to thee?" This he could not
do. He struck hands with the German,
had a mass said to St. Michael, took his
daughter — and lo! he was coming to
America.

The journey was not as pleasant as he
expected. In Hamburg they robbed him
of the greater part of his money; on the
ship he was crowded with the rest of the
steerage passengers. The rolling of the ship
and the vast expanse of the ocean frightened him. No one could understand him,
nor he any one. He was bundled
around like baggage; they pushed him
aside like the stone by the wayside; the
Germans made fun of him. At dinner-
time, when they all pressed with their
tin pans to the cook, who was distributing

food, they pushed him to the end of the line, so that sometimes he did not get enough to eat, and was hungry. On the steamer he felt strange, lonely, and sad. He felt that no one cared for him except God. In the presence of his daughter he tried to look cheerful, cocked his cap on one side, called her attention to everything new, marvelled himself, but trusted in nothing. At moments he was apprehensive that perhaps these "heathen," as he called his fellow-travelers, would cast him into the sea or command him to change his religion, or to sign some paper, perhaps, even a "*cyrograf!*"—to sell his soul to the devil.

The steamer went forward day and night over the unfathomable sea—shook, groaned, and churned the water into foam, breathed as a dragon, and at night emitted a long tail of fiery sparks, so that it seemed to him like some suspicious and uncanny force. These childish fears, although he did not confess them, oppressed his heart; for this Polish peasant, torn from his native nest, was truly a helpless child, and verily under the care of God alone. His head and heart could not contain all that he saw and felt; so it was not strange that as he was sitting on the coil of rope his head was bent under his burden of heavy trouble and uncertainty. The sea-breezes sang in his ears and kept repeating, "Lipintse! Lipintse!" Sometimes it whistled like a Polish flute. The sun spoke to him: "How do you do, Lorenz? I was in Lipintse." But the screw of the propeller churned the water more violently and the smokestack sent forth great clouds of smoke, and these two were like some evil spirits who carried him farther and farther from Lipintse.

Meanwhile Mary was troubled by other thoughts and memories, and they followed

her like the foamy-way behind the ship,
or the flying sea-gulls. She recalled how
last autumn, late one evening, shortly before their departure, she went to the old
well in Lipintse to draw some water. The
first stars twinkled in the sky. She was
singing as she drew up the bucket:

> "John watered the horses,
>   Kassya drew the water,"

and she was as sad as the swallow who
twitters mournfully before its flight to
the south. Then from the dark woods
came the long note of the ligavka, which
was the signal of John Smolak, the hostler,
to let her know that he would soon
come.

Presently the sound of hoofs was heard,
and he rode up to the well, jumped from
the stallion's back, shook his flaxen-col-
ored locks, and now the memory of his
words was as music to her ears. She

closed her eyes, and it seemed that Smolak whispered again to her in his trembling voice:

" If thy father is so obstinate, then I too will give up my place, dispose of my property, and follow thee. My Mary, where thou wilt be, there too shall I fly like a stork in the air, float as a duck on the lake, roll as a golden hoop on the road, and find you, my own! What is my lot without thee? Where thou wilt go, there I will follow. Thy fate will be my fate; together we shall live, and together we shall die. And as I vowed to thee over this well, so let God forsake me, if I forsake thee, Mary, my only love."

Recalling these words, Mary saw the well, and the large red moon over the tops of the woods, and John, as if he were alive.

These thoughts cheered her and eased her burden. John was a determined

youth, so she believed that what he said
he would do. Now she wished only that
he could be by her side and listen with
her to the sounds of the sad sea. She
would be glad and happy then, because he
feared no one and knew how to take care
of himself. What was he doing now in
Lipintse, where likely the first snow had
fallen? Did he go to the woods with his
ax, or did he care for his horses, or was
he sent on an errand with his sleigh, or
did he cut openings in the ice? Where
was the dear one now? Here the girl, in
her mind's eye, saw Lipintse as it was:
the crackling snow on the road, the red
sky, between black, leafless branches, the
cawing flocks of crows, the chimney
smoke rising to the sky, the frozen sweep
of the well, and in the distance the
forest sprinkled with snow and reddened
by the setting sun.

Ah! where is she now? Where will her

father take her? As far as the eye can
reach, nothing but water and water. The
greenish furrows and foamy billows on
these immeasurable watery fields, this one
ship—a strayed bird: skies above, desert
below, great voices of the crying waves
and whistling winds, and there in front
of the vessel's prow, somewhere afar off,
on the edge of the world—land.

Alas, John! how will you find her
there? Will you fly through the air like
a falcon? will you swim through the
water like a fish? and do you in Lipintse
think of her?

Slowly the sun lowered to the west
and was falling into the ocean. On the
ripples of the waves a bright pathway was
spread out, embroidered with golden
scales; it coruscated, flashed, shone,
burned and merged in the sunlight in the
distance. The ship, entering into this

fiery pathway, seemed to chase the setting sun.

The escaping smoke from the funnel became red, the sails and wet ropes pink. The sailors began to sing; the ruddy disk looked larger and larger, and was slowly sinking into the sea. Soon you could only see half of its orb above the waves, and then the whole west was flooded with one great glow, and in this glorious brightness you could not tell where ended the luster of the waves, and where began the sky, air, and firmament, all saturated in this radiance, which at last gradually becoming tenderer, the ocean murmured in one long, low pean, as if intoning its evening prayers.

In moments like these the soul gets wings; what it has to remember, it remembers; what it loves, it loves still more warmly; what it longs for, there it flies.

Lorenz and Mary both felt, that though
the wind carried them as useless leaves,
the tree which gave them birth is not the
land to which they go, but that from
whence they came: that Polish land,
which is so fruitful, swaying like one
great field of golden grain, covered with
green forests, dotted with thatched roofs,
full of meadows golden with buttercups,
and blue with lakes swarming with storks
and swallows, with its wayside crosses and
the white villas among the linden trees:
where one is greeted with "The Lord be
praised," and answers "For ever and
ever," the most worshipful, the sweetest
mother, so upright, so beloved, and above
all in the world. So what these peasant
hearts had not felt before they now felt.
Lorenz removed his cap and the western
light fell on his gray hair. His thoughts
were busy; the poor fellow did not know

how to express his feelings to his daughter.   At last he said to her:

"Mary, it seems to me as if we had left something behind us."

"Fortune is left and love is left," faintly answered the girl, lifting her eyes as if in prayer.

Meanwhile it became darker, the passengers began to leave the deck, signs of commotion could be seen on the ship. The night is not always quiet after a beautiful sunset; therefore the whistles of the mates sounded continually and the sailors hauled on the ropes.   The last purple reflection died out on the sea, and from the water arose a mist; a few stars flickered in the sky, then disappeared; the mist visibly thickened, enveloping the sky, horizon, and the ship itself; the smoke-stack and the great masts could yet be seen; the figures of the mariners from afar looked like shadows; an hour later, all,

even the lights which had been hung on
the tops of the masts and the sparks which
the funnel breathed out, were hidden in a
white fog.

The ship did not roll. The waves became weaker, then fainter, and glided
smoothly away under the heavy fog.

The night was falling blind and still.
Suddenly, among the stillness from the
far-off horizon, came the echoes of mys-
terious voices. They were like the heavy
breathing of approaching giants. At times
it seemed as if some one called from the
darkness, and from a distance came a cho-
rus of voices, immeasurably sad and
mournful, as if repining and lamenting.
These calls seemed to come from the
boundless infinitude of the gray night.

The sailors, hearing the murmuring of
these voices, say that it is the god of storm
calling the winds from hell.

The indications of the storm became

more and more apparent. The captain,
clad in a mackintosh and an oilskin cap
upon his head, stood on the highest bridge;
the mate stood in the usual place by the
compass. There were no passengers on
the deck. Lorenz with Mary had de-
scended to the steerage compartment. Silence reigned there. The lights of the
lamps fastened in the low ceiling burned
dimly; the emigrants sat in groups near
the bunks in the walls. The hall was
large, but gloomy, as steerages generally
are. The bunks rose in tiers close to the
roof, looking like the dark lairs of animals, and the whole gave one the impres-
sion of a dark, murky wine-cellar. The
air was filled with the smells of sailcloth,
tarred ropes, bilge water, and dampness.
Does anything here remind you of the
handsome saloons of the cabin passengers?
Even two weeks in such a hole poisons the
lungs with its unwholesome air, covers the

skin with a sickly pallor, and often breeds
scurvy.

Lorenz and Mary had been there only
four days, and if you would compare the
Mary from Lipintse, healthy and rosy,
with the Mary of to-day, wan and pale,
you would hardly recognize her.   Old Lorenz had also become as yellow as wax,
which was aggravated because they had
not come on deck the first two days of the
passage: they thought that it was not al-
lowed.   How could they know what was
permitted and what prohibited?   They
simply wore afraid to move or leave their
baggage.   Now they and all the rest, sat
by their things, and the whole place was
littered over with the bundles of the emigrants, which increased the disorder and
the disheartening aspect.   Mattresses,
clothing, packages of food, tools, tin cups,
and platters lay in heaps upon the floor.
Upon them sat the emigrants, nearly all

Germans. Some chewed tobacco, some
smoked pipes; the puffs of smoke struck
the ceiling, then spread in wide layers, dim-
ming the lamplight. A few children cried
in the corners, but the crowd had ceased
their usual noise, because the fog infused
everything with uneasiness and anxiety.
The more experienced travelers knew that
this foretold a storm. It was no secret
that danger and perhaps death was approaching. Lorenz and Mary could not
make out anything, though when the
hatchway was opened for a moment they
could distinctly hear those ominous voices,
coming from afar.

They both sat in the narrowest part,
near the bow; the annoying motion of the
ship was more perceptible here, and that
was the reason why their fellow-passengers
had crowded them there. The old man
strengthened himself with bread from Li-

pintse, and the girl, who was tired of doing nothing, braided her hair for the night.

This unusual silence, interrupted only by the children's cries, surprised her.

"Why do the Germans sit so still?" asked she.

"Do I know?" answered Lorenz.   "It may be some holy day with them."

Suddenly the ship shook terribly, as if it trembled before something frightful. The tin utensils rattled against each other, the lamp flames jumped and flashed brighter, and a few frightened voices began to ask:

"What is that?   What is it?"

But there was no answer.

A second shock, stronger than the first, jarred the vessel; its bow rose up quickly in the air and as quickly plowed into the trough of the sea, and the waves dashed heavily against the windward portholes.

"The storm is coming," whispered Mary in a frightened voice.

Meanwhile the tempest roared around the ship like a whirlwind through a forest —howled like a pack of yelling wolves. The sharp wind struck again and again, careening the vessel, tossing it up on the crest of the waves and casting it down into the depths. The bedding, tools, tin pans, and packages were thrown from one corner to another. Some of the emigrants were knocked off their feet. The feathers from the pillows flew about, and the chimneys rattled on the lamps.

Then the air resounded with the noise and clatter of the waves dashing on the deck, the quivering and jarring of the ship, the cries of the women and children, and amid this chaos could be heard the shrill whistle of the officers and the tramping of the sailors running overhead.

"Virgin of the Bright Mountain!" whispered Mary.

The bow of the ship, where they were, flew madly up and down, and despite the fact that they were holding on to their bunks, they were often thrown against the sides. The roar of the tempest increased, and the creaking of the beams and bolts became so frightful that it seemed as if they would part with a great crash.

"Hold tight, Mary!" cried her father, trying to overcome the noise of the storm; but soon a great fear clutched them by the throat. In their terror the children stopped their crying, and the women their weeping: they all breathed quickly, and hands eagerly grasped fixed objects. The fury of the storm waxed stronger; the elements cut loose. The fog mixed with the darkness, the clouds with the water, the wind with the spray; the waves striking the ship like the concussion of cannon

balls, threw it to the right, to the left—
from the clouds even to the bottom of the
ocean. Sometimes the foamy manes of
the waves washed over the whole length
of the ship, gigantic walls of water seethed,
hissed, and boiled in a terrific commotion.

The oil lamps flickered and one by one
went out. It became darker and darker,
and to Lorenz and Mary it seemed that
the darkness of death was approaching.

"Mary," began the peasant in a broken
voice, for he lacked breath, "Mary, forgive
me, that I brought thee to perdition. Our
last hour has come. We shall never again
look with our sinful eyes on this world.
Not for us confession, not for us extreme
unction, not for us to lie in our graves,
but only from the waters to rise on the
last judgment day, my poor one!"

When he so spoke Mary understood that
there was no help for them. Different

thoughts flew through her head and her soul cried out:

"John! my John with the golden heart! do you in Lipintse hear me now?" And this cruel grief so oppressed her heart that she began to weep loudly. The noise of her weeping could be heard in the place, which was as silent as a funeral. One voice cried out from the corner, "Be still!" and then stopped, as if frightened by its own sound. Another lamp chimney fell to the floor, and the flame went out, and it became still darker. The people huddled together, so as to be near one another. Fear and silence ruled everywhere. Presently could be heard the voice of Lorenz:

"Kyrie eleison."

"Christe eleison," answered Mary, weeping.

"Christ hear us."

"God, the Father in heaven, have mercy upon us."

They both repeated the Litany. In this dark compartment the voice of the old man and the answers of the maiden, broken by her sobs, sounded with great solemnity. Some of the emigrants uncovered their heads. Gradually the sobbing of the maiden ceased; their voices became more quiet and clear, and the storm outside shrieked as if in accompaniment.

A cry of terror broke from the group near the hatchway; an immense wave dashed in the door and flooded the compartment; the water rushed hissing into all corners; the women began to shriek and climb into the bunks. It appeared to all that the end had come.

Shortly there entered an officer, with a lantern in his hand, his clothes dripping with water and with flushed face.

In a few words he quieted the women,

saying the water got in by accident, and
then he added that because the ship was
on the open sea there was but little danger.
Thus an hour or two passed. The storm
still raged. The ship creaked, labored,
rolled, careened, but still it rode the
waves. The passengers' fears were allayed
and some went to sleep. A few hours
more passed, and into the dark compartment through the grated skylight filtered
the gray break of day. The morning
broke pale on the ocean, as if frightened,
sad, and gloomy; but it brought some
cheer and hope. Having said all the
prayers they knew by heart, Lorenz and
Mary climbed into their bunks and slept
soundly.

They were awakened by the sound of
the bell that called them to breakfast.
But they could not eat. Their heads were
as heavy as lead. The old man felt worse
than Mary; he could get nothing through

his confused head.   The German who had
enticed him to come to America had said
that he would have to cross the water, but
he never thought that the water was so
wide and that it would take so many days
and nights to cross it.   He thought he
would cross it on a ferryboat, as he had
crossed a river.   If he had known that the
sea was so large, he would have remained
in Lipintse.   Besides, one other thought
disturbed him: had he not led his own and
his daughter's soul to perdition'   Was it
not a sin for a Catholic from Lipintse to
tempt the Lord God by committing himself to the abysses of water on which he
has now been five days, crossing to another
coast, if there be another coast at all?
His doubts and fears had seven days more
to increase.

The   storm   raged   forty-eight hours,
then it abated.   Mary and he felt encour-
aged to venture on deck again; but when

they saw the immense waves rolling yet,
dark and angry, the huge mountains of
water approaching the ship, and the gulfs
beneath, they again thought that only a
divine hand, or some other power not
human, could save them from those
depths.

At last it cleared up.   Day after day
passed, and they could see only water and
water without end, sometimes green,
sometimes blue, merging into the sky.
Upon that sky there frequently floated
small, bright clouds, which reddened at
evening, and laid themselves down to
sleep in the far west.   The ship chased
them on the water.   Lorenz, indeed,
thought that perhaps the sea would never
end, but took courage and decided to
ask.

Once, taking off his cap and bowing
low to a passing sailor, he said:

"Your honor, will we soon arrive?"

For a wonder, the sailor did not burst out laughing, but stood and listened. On his weather-beaten face could be seen an expression, as if he was recalling the past, and was struggling to see it clearly. Then, speaking in German, he said:

"*Was?*"

"Will we soon arrive, your honor?"

"Two days, two days," said the sailor in Polish, with difficulty, at the same time holding up two fingers.

"I humbly thank you."

"Where do you come from?"

"From Lipintse."

"*Was ist das Lipintse?*"

Mary, who had come forward when they were speaking, blushed deeply, and lifting her eyes bashfully, said in a modest voice:

"We are from Poznan."

The sailor looked musingly at a brass nail in the rail; then he looked at the girl, on her bright flaxen hair, and one could have seen by his bronzed face that he was affected. Shortly he said gravely:

"I am from Dantzic—I understand Polish—I am Kaszub—your *bruder*, but that was long ago. *Jetzt bin ich Deutsch.*"

After he had said that he turned his back, and lifting the end of a rope, cried out, sailor-fashion "Yo-hoy!" and began pulling on it.

From that time, whenever he saw Lorenz or Mary he smiled at them in a friendly manner. They were very glad that they had found one kindly soul on this German ship, and that their journey would soon be over.

The next morning when they went on the deck a strange sight met their eyes. They saw something floating on the water, and when they came nearer they saw it was a large, red barrel, rocking gently on the waves; in the distance, reaching out, were a number of others. The sea and air were veiled in a slight mist; they looked mild and silvery, the surface was smooth and still, and as far as the eye could reach could be observed more barrels. There were great quantities of sea-gulls following the ship with their cries. There was unusual commotion on the deck. The sailors had changed their clothes, some of them washed the deck, and others polished the brass work. From the mast they hung a flag, and from the stern another.

All the passengers seemed cheerful and animated, and every one came on deck. Some brought up their baggage and began to strap it.

Seeing all this confusion Mary said: " Now we shall certainly reach the land."

They became more cheerful. Then in

the west could be discerned Sandy Hook,
then an island with a building on it, and
then, in the distance, something like
dense, fog-like clouds or smoke, stretched
on the water, indistinct, far, mixed, form-
less.   At this sight a great babel of voices
arose; they all pointed with their fingers;
the ship whistled shrilly as if from joy.

" What is that?" inquired Lorenz.

" New York," answered Kaszub, who
was standing near by.

Then the mist and smoke lifted and disappeared, and in the background, as the
ship was cutting through the silvery
water, could be seen the outlines of
houses, roofs and chimneys; the church
steeples and high buildings were painted
more clearly against the blue.   In the
lower part of the city could be seen forests
of masts, from which floated thousands of
vari-colored flags, which swayed in the
breeze like flowers upon the meadow.

The ship came nearer and nearer—the beautiful city arose as if from the water. Lorenz, who was filled with astonishment and joy, took off his cap, opened wide his mouth and looked, then said to his daughter:

"Mary."

"Well?"

"Do you see it?"

"I do."

"Do you marvel?"

"I do marvel."

Lorenz not only wondered, but he coveted. Seeing the green shores on both sides of the bay, the darker green of the uplands, the cultivated lawns and grounds, he spoke again:

"Bless the Lord! If they would give me land near the city, with that meadow, it would be nearer to the market, and I could drive the cow and hogs to the fair. There must be multitudes of people here.

In Poland I was a peasant, but here I shall be a large land-owner."

At this moment the long stretches of Staten Island spread out before him in all its beauty. Lorenz, seeing groves of trees, said again:

"I shall bow low to the government officer, shall speak deftly to him and ask him for about eighty acres of these woods for my 'inheritance.' In the morning I will send my hired man into the city with the wood. Glory to the Highest! for I now see that my German did not cheat me."

Mary also was dreaming of "inheritance," and she did not know why a song that the bridesmaids sing to the grooms in Lipintse came into her head. In this song the maidens tell the young men that all they possess is their tasseled caps and embroidered coats. Perhaps she intends to sing such a song to poor John, when he arrives—when she will be rich.

Meanwhile the quarantine tug had arrived. Four or five people came on board. Then came another boat from the city, bringing agents from hotels and boarding-houses, guides, money-changers and railroad agents. Then arose a great clamor; they pushed and jostled among the passengers. Lorenz and Mary were caught in this vortex and knew not what to do.

Kaszub, the friendly sailor, helped the old man to change his money; he obtained forty-seven dollars in silver for all that he had. Before this had ended the ship came so close to the city that they could see not only the houses, but even the people at Battery Park; then it passed near a number of vessels, large and small, and at last reached the wharf and glided into a narrow dock.

Their journey was ended.

The passengers began to swarm from the ship, like bees from a hive; they crowded the narrow gangway and collected in groups on the dock: first-class, then second, and at last the steerage passengers loaded with their luggage. When Lorenz and Mary, pushed by the crowd, reached the exit, there Kaszub met them and squeezing Lorenz's hand said:

"*Bruder*, I wish you good luck, and to you, miss, God help you."

"God repay you," they both answered, but there was no time for further speech. The crowd pushed them forward on the gangway to the large inclosure.

The customs officer with his silver shield pinched and prodded their bundles, said "All right," and pointed to the doorway. They went out and found themselves on the streets.

"Father, what shall we do now?" asked Mary.

"We should wait here. The German said that a government officer will come and ask for us."

So they stood, leaning against the wall, waiting for him, with the noise of the great unknown city surrounding them. They had never seen anything like it before. The streets ran straight and wide, with crowds of people upon them, like at fair time in Poland; in the middle were street cars and on the sides wagons, carriages and omnibuses. Around them they heard a strange kind of speech; the workmen and drivers cried out to each other. Often some black people with short woolly hair would pass them. Seeing them, Lorenz and Mary devoutly crossed themselves. This city appeared strange, full of din and noise, whistles, the rattling of wagons, and the cries and shouts of the people. Everybody went so quickly that they looked as if they were either chasing, or trying to escape from, somebody, and besides, what an ant-hill of people, what strange faces—some dark, some bronzed, some olive. There they stood near the docks, where ships were loading and unloading, where it was very crowded and busy; the wagons rattled, the trucks groaned, and the noise reminded them of a sawmill.

In this way passed an hour—another— and they still stood by the wall, waiting for the officer.

A strange sight they presented to the large city of New York—this Polish peasant, with his long grayish hair and four cornered lambskin cap, and this maiden from Lipintse, dressed in a dark-blue cotton dress, and strings of beads around her neck.

Yet people passed them without looking at them. New faces or strange dresses do not surprise New Yorkers.

Another hour passed; the sky became overcast; rain and sleet began to fall; a cold moist wind came from the water.

They still stood, waiting for the officer.

The peasant nature is patient; but somehow uneasiness began to creep into their souls.

They had felt lonely on the ship among strangers, and on the wide watery wastes sick and fearful. They had prayed to God that he would lead them, as lost children, through the dangers of the sea. They had thought that as soon as they landed their woes would be ended. Now they had arrived, were in the midst of this great city, but in this city with its noise and din they suddenly felt that they were still more lonely and afraid than they had been on the steamer.

The officer had not arrived. What would they do if he should never come, if the German had deceived them?

At this thought their poor peasant hearts quaked with fear.   What would they do? Simply—perish.

Meanwhile the wind blew through their clothing and the rain beat in their faces.

"Mary, are you cold?" inquired Lorenz.

"I am, father," replied she.

Another hour was tolled by the city clock.   It was getting dusky.   The crowds were becoming thinner, and the dock laborers were leaving; the lamps on the streets were lighted, and a great sea of light flooded the city.   Gradually Battery Park became deserted.   The Emigrant Office was closed.

They stood waiting for the officer.

At last night had fallen and the docks became silent.   From time to time the black funnels of the ferryboats sent forth clouds of sparks, which went out in the darkness, and the waves splashed against the stone embankment.   Sometimes was

heard the song of a drunken sailor, returning to his ship; the lamp lights began to
flicker in the mist.   They waited.

Even if they concluded not to wait,
where could they go? what could they do?
where could they turn, and where could
they lay their weary heads? The cold
pierced them sharply, and hunger gnawed
at their vitals. If they had only a roof
above their heads, for they were wet to
the skin! Ah! the officer did not come—
he would not come, for such an officer
did not exist. The German was a steamship ticket agent, who received commis-
sions from his sales, and cared for nothing more.

Lorenz felt that his feet were getting
numb, that some great weight pressed
upon him, as if the wrath of God hung
over him.

He waited patiently as only a peasant
can. The voice of his daughter, shiver-

ing from the cold, awoke him, as if from
a dream.

"Father."

" Still.   No mercy for us."

" Let us return to Lipintse."

" Don't be foolish."

" My God! my God!" silently whispered Mary.

Lorenz was overcome with grief.

" My poor child!   If God only had
mercy on thee!"

But she did not hear.   Leaning her
head against the wall, she closed her eyes
and fell into an uneasy, feverish sleep;
and in her dreams she seemed to see and
hear, pictured as in a frame, Lipintse and
the sound of her John's voice, singing
mockingly:

" What a fine lady!   What a fine lady!
Thy trousseau is only a garland of daisies."

The first light of day fell upon the

water, upon the masts, and upon the Emigrant building.

In this gray light could be seen two figures, sleeping by the wall, with blue, pale faces, covered with snow and motionless, as if dead.   But in their book of woe only the first leaves were turned.

CHAPTER II.

IN NEW YORK.

IN New York, starting from Broadway
in the direction of Chatham Square and
crossing several streets, the traveler meets
a part of the city more and more poor,
neglected, and squalid. The streets are
very narrow. The houses, built, perhaps,
by the Dutch colonists, have become
cracked and warped with old age: the
roofs have sunk in, the plaster has dropped
from the walls, and the walls themselves
have so settled that the cellar windows are
level with the street. Strange crooked
lines have taken the place of the usual
straight American streets: uneven walls,
and roofs crowd and terrace one upon

another with their broken slates and shingles.

In wet weather pools of water stand in the streets, muddy and thick. The windows of the dilapidated houses look down upon these puddles, in which can be seen pieces of paper, pasteboard, glass, wood, and clippings of tin: the streets, or rather their layers of mud, are littered with this rubbish; everywhere can be seen dirt, filth, disorder, and human misery.

In these quarters are boarding-houses, where one can live for two dollars a week; also saloons, where they entice unfortunate men to go on whaling vessels; secret agents from Venezuela, Ecuador, and Brazil, who persuade people to colonize the tropics and who furnish the yellow fever with quantities of victims; restaurants, who feed their guests on salt meat, rotten oysters and fish, that perhaps are cast up on the beach by the water; private

gambling houses, Chinese laundries, mariners' rests and dens of crime, misery,
hunger, tears.

And yet this part of the big city is
crowded, for all emigrants who cannot
find even temporary lodgings in Castle
Garden gather here, dwell, live, and die.
Also, it could be said, that if immigration
consists of the refuse of Europe, the deni-
zens of this neighborhood consist of the
refuse of immigration. The people are
idle here, partly for want of work, but
mostly because they like it. At night can
often be heard the report of revolvers, cries
for help, hoarse shouts of rage, the songs
of drunken sailors, or the brawls of quar-
reling negroes. In the daytime the groups
of ragged loafers, with pipes in their
mouths, crowd around a street fight.
Children, white and black, instead of
being at school, play in the streets and
throw banana peels at each other; emaci-

ated beggar women hold out their hands
to the better dressed people who happen
to pass.

In such a human Gehenna we find our
two old friends, Lorenz Toporek and his
daughter Mary.   The "inheritance"
which they expected was a dream and
passed as a dream, and the reality appears
in the form of a narrow basement room,
deep in the ground, with one window,
partly broken; from the walls of the room
oozes unhealthy slime and streaks of moisture; by the wall stands a rusty and dilapidated stove and a table with three legs; a
pile of straw in the corner serves as a bed;
that is all.   Old Lorenz, kneeling in
front of the stove, tries to find a potato in
the cold ashes; he has not eaten for two
days.   Mary sits on the straw with her
hands clasped around her knees and stares
motionless.   The girl is thin and ill.   It
is the same Mary, but her rosy cheeks are

now sunken; her color is pale and sickly, her face looks smaller than before, and her eyes are large and vacant. On her face can be seen the effects of foul air, care, and insufficient food.

They lived only on potatoes, but for two days even these were lacking. They were at a loss what to do or how to live. It was at the end of the third month that they had lived in this hole, and their money was gone. Old Lorenz had tried to get work, but no one understood what he wanted. He went to the docks to load coal upon the ships, but he had no wheel-barrow; besides, an Irishman had given him a black eye; he could get no work around buildings, because he had no tools; and a workman is of no use who does not understand what is said to him; whatever he undertook or wherever he went they laughed at him, pushed him about, and often beat him; so he could find nothing

to do and he could not get or earn any
money.   His hair had become white from
anxiety; hope was dead, his money was
gone, and hunger began.

In his country, among his own, if he
had lost his all, if sickness had ruined
him, or his children had put him out of
the house, he would have taken a staff in
his hand and would have stood under a
cross by the wayside or at the entrance of
some church and sung for alms.   The
gentlemen passing that way would give
him a dime, the lady would send from her
carriage her little daughter, with her great
pitying eyes and money in her pink hands;
a peasant would give him a loaf of bread
and a woman a slice of bacon, and he
could live, as a bird who neither sows nor
plows.   Besides, if he had stood under the
cross, its guarding arms would spread
above him, the skies would be overhead
and the fields around, and in this silence

of nature the Lord God would hear his songs. But in this great city, that hummed like a mighty engine, everybody rushed onward and looked only ahead, so that they could not see the suffering of others. The head swam here, the arms drooped, the eyes were bewildered with the many sights, and the thoughts chased each other; everything was so strange and repelling, whirling at full speed, so that they who did not know how to revolve in this wheel were cast out and broken like an earthen jar.

Ah me! what a difference there is here! In quiet Lipintse Lorenz had some land, he was respected by his neighbors, was sure of his living; every Sunday he went to church and offered a candle; and here he was lost among all, like a stray dog in a strange yard—timid, trembling, bent, and hungry. In his first days of suffering memory said to him: " It was better for

thee in Lipintse." His conscience cried:
"Lorenz, why did you leave Lipintse?"
Why? because God had deserted him.
The peasant would carry his cross, would
willingly suffer, if there would only be an
end to his suffering; but he knew well that
every day there would be a greater trial,
and every morning the sun would shine
upon the increasing misery of himself and
daughter. What would he do? Would
he make a rope, say a prayer, and hang
himself? When he thought what would
become of his daughter he felt that not
only God had forsaken him, but that even
his reason was leaving him. There was
no light in this darkness, and his greatest
pain he even could not name.

This was the longing for Lipintse. It
tortured him day and night; this torture
became so much more frightful because he
was unconscious of what he wanted, and
it was tugging at his peasant's heart, like

a dog at its chain, while he writhed in
agony. What he needed was the pine forests, the fields, and cottages thatched with
straw, the gentry, peasants and priests,
and all that, above which his native sky
was hanging and from which the heart, if
once attached, cannot break away, and,
when it breaks, drips with blood. The
peasant felt as if something weighed him
to the earth. At times he felt like tearing
his hair, butting his head against the wall,
casting himself on the ground and crying
aloud for some one in his frenzy. Now
he is bent under his terrible burden, he is
sinking, and still the hum of this strange
city sings in his ears; he groans and calls
on the Divine Lord; here there is no cross,
no one answers him, but the hum of the
city goes on, and upon the straw pallet
there sits the girl with eyes staring into
vacancy—hungry, and suffering silently.
It is a strange thing that, although the

girl and he were constantly together, so
benumbed by misery were they that often
for whole days they never spoke to each
other. Sad and miserable were their lives.
What had they to speak of ? The open
wounds had better be left untouched.
Will they then say that they have no more
money, that there are no more potatoes,
no more ideas in their heads?

Help they get from none. Many Poles
live in New York, but the well-to-do never
live in the vicinity of Chatham Square.
The second week after their arrival they
got acquainted with two Polish families,
one from Silesia and one from Poznan,
but they were suffering themselves. Two
of the Silesian children died, a third one
was ill, and yet for two weeks it had been
sleeping with its parents under an arch of
the bridge. They existed on what they
could pick out of the garbage barrels.
Later they were taken to a hospital, and it

was not known what had become of them.
The second family was equally unhappy
and even in a still worse condition, for the
father of the family was a drunkard.
Mary tried to help the woman as long as
she could, but now she herself needed
help. Truly they might have gone to the
Polish Catholic Church in Hoboken, and
the priest would have let others know of
them, but they did not know that there
was any Polish church or priest; they had
no one to tell them of it. In this way
every cent they spent was a step on the
stairs leading into the gulf of misery.

At this moment they sat, he by the
stove and she on the straw. One hour
passed, then another. The room was getting darker and darker, though it was
only noontime; a mist arose from the
water as it does usually in the spring—
heavy, chilly, and penetrating. Both
shivered with the cold: at last, Lorenz

gave up his search for a potato in the ashes.

"Mary," said he, "I can't stand this any longer, neither can you. I will go to the water to pick up some wood: we can then make a fire and perhaps I may find something to eat."

She said nothing, so he went out. He had learned to go to the docks and pick up pieces of board that had been thrown in the water, as do all those who have no money to buy coal. Sometimes he would find some vegetables and bananas floating on the water that had been thrown from the fruiterers. When he was busy with this occupation he would momentarily forget his misery and the longing that consumed him. It was lunch-time when he came to the dock, and some boys who were near the edge of the water commenced to plague and jeer him, throwing pieces of coal and sticks at him. There

were pieces of broken boxes floating of
the water; one wave would bring them
near him and then they would recede
from him, but soon he managed to secure
enough.

Something green floated on the water:
perhaps it was something to eat, but being
light it did not come near the shore, and
he could not reach it. The boys had a
sinker fastened to the end of a line,
which they threw beyond these objects
and thus pulled them ashore: ho had no
line, so he looked covetously, and waiting
until the boys had gone ho looked over
their leavings and ate what he thought
was fit. At this moment he forgot that
Mary had not eaten.

Luck now smiled on him. Returning
home he met a wagon filled with potatoes,
which had stuck on the street, and the
horses were unable to move it. Lorenz
grasped one of the spokes of the wheel

and helped the driver to start. It was so
heavy that he felt the strain on his back,
but at last they started, and some potatoes fell on the ground. The driver did
not stop to pick them up, thanked
Lorenz for his help and went off.

Lorenz gathered them with trembling
hands, hid them in his breast and felt
more cheerful. A piece of bread, found
at the time of hunger, gives happiness.
The peasant, returning home, muttered,
" Thanks be to God, that he looked upon
our distress: the wood is found, the girl
will make a fire; the potatoes will last for
two meals. The Lord God is merciful!
Our room will be warm. Mary has not
eaten for two days. She will be glad.
The Lord God is merciful!"

Muttering thus to himself, he carried
the boards with one hand, and with the
other felt that his potatoes were safe. He
was bringing great treasures, so he lifted

his eyes with gratitude to heaven and muttered again:

"I thought I should steal them; and now, without stealing, they fell from the wagon; we shall eat now. The Lord God is merciful! Mary will arise from the straw when she finds out that I have potatoes."

Mary had not moved from the time he left the room. Previously, in the morning, when Lorenz had brought wood, she made the fire, boiled water, ate what they had, and for whole hours watched the blaze. She, also, had sought for work. She was hired once in a boarding-house to wash dishes and sweep, but was discharged in two days, because she did not understand the orders; she was discouraged and did not try again. For whole days she sat in the house, fearing to go on the streets, because Irishmen and drunken sailors insulted her. This idleness increased her misery. The longing gnawed her, as rust does iron. She was more unhappy than Lorenz, because to hunger, to the conviction that there was no help for them, no escape, no to-morrow, to the terrible longing for Lipintse, the thought of John added its additional weight. Had he not vowed to her and said: "Where thou shalt go, there I will go?" She had come to America to receive her "inheritance" and be a lady, and now how all had changed!

He was working on a gentleman's estate, and besides had the small property left him by his father, while she was as poor and as hungry as a rat in the church in Lipintse. Will he ever come? and if he comes, will he take her to his bosom and say: "My poor dear sufferer," or "Leave me, thou pauper's daughter?" What is now her trousseau?—rags. The dogs would bark at her now in Lipintse, and yet something draws her there, and oh, her soul would be glad to leave her and fly there, as a swallow on the water.

John is there, remembering or not remembering, but very dear to her; only by his side would be peace, joy, and gladness, of all men, only by his side alone.

When they had a fire in the stove, and the hunger did not gripe them as badly as now, the flames—hissing, shooting sparks, jumping, flickering—spoke to her of Lipintse and reminded her how she had sat with other girls spinning. John, peeping out from another room, cried out: "Mary, let us go to a priest, for thou art dear to to me." She answered him: "Be quiet, John;" and she felt joy in her soul, as she did when he took her on the floor to dance with him, and she, shielding her eyes, would whisper: "Leave me, for I feel ashamed." When the flames recalled all this, the tears would trickle down her

face; but now there was neither fire in the
stove nor tears in her eyes, for she had
shed them all. Sometimes it seemed to
her that they flooded her breast and choked
her. Sometimes she felt a great weariness
and exhaustion, and she was too weak to
think; but she suffered patiently, looking
before her with her large eyes, like a bird
that is tortured.

In this way she now looked, sitting on
the straw. Some one opened the door.
Mary, thinking that it was her father, did
not lift her head, when a strange voice
said:

"Look here!"

He was the proprietor of the den where
they lived, an old mulatto with a gloomy
and repulsive face, shabby and dirty, with
a chew of tobacco in his mouth.

Seeing him, the girl was very frightened. They had to pay a dollar for the
next week, and they had not a cent. She

hoped to mollify him by being humble, so she came to him and kissed his hand.

"I came for my money," he said.

She understood the word "money," and shaking her head and trying to speak, at the same time looking supplicatingly, she gave him to understand that they had none, that for two days they had not eaten, that they were hungry, and that he should have mercy upon them.

"God will pay you, honorable gentleman," she added in Polish, at a loss to do or speak more.

The "honorable gentleman" did not understand that he was honorable, but he guessed that he would not get his dollar; guessed even so well that he gathered their bundles in one arm, and with his other hand he took the g'rl by the arm and led her from the room, and giving her a push up the stairs, conducted her to the street, and, throwing her things at her feet, with

equal unconcern opened the door of an
adjoining saloon and called out:

"Hi! Pat, I have a room for you."

"All right," answered a voice from the
inside, "I will come to-night."

The mulatto disappeared in the dark
hallway, leaving the girl standing on the
street.   She put her bundles in a corner
of the wall, so that they would be out of
the mud, and, standing near them, waited
patiently and silently, as usual.

The drunken sailor on passing by did
not touch her this time.   Although it had
been dark in the room, on the street it was
quite light, and in this light the face of
the girl appeared quite emaciated, as if
after some severe illness.   Only her bright
flaxen hair remained the same, but her
lips were blue, her eyes feverish.   She
looked like a flower that, wilting, is slowly
dying.

The passers-by looked at her with pity.

An old negress asked her something, but receiving no reply, went on, feeling offended.

Meanwhile Lorenz was wending his way homeward with feelings that are often awakened in the poor by the visible proof of divine mercy. He now had potatoes; he thought how they would taste, how to-morrow he would again help the drivers, and of the time after the to morrow he did not think, because he was very hungry. Seeing the girl standing on the pavement in front of the house, he was very much surprised, and hastened his steps.

"Why art thou standing here?"

"The landlord has put us out, father."

"Put us out?"

The wood fell from the peasant's hands. This was too much for him. To expell them at this time, when they had wood and potatoes! What would they do now? Where would they cook? How would

they strengthen themselves? Where would
they go? Taking his cap from his head,
he threw it on the ground by the wood.
"Lord! Lord!" He turned round, opened
his mouth, and looking on the girl with a
dazed look, repeated once more:

"Put us out?"

He turned, as if to walk off, then
stopped, and with a husky and severe
voice, said:

"Why did you not supplicate him, you
stupid?"

She sighed.

"I did."

"Did you kiss his hand?"

"I did."

Lorenz turned round again in the same
spot, as a worm that is pierced through,
and everything became dark before his
eyes.

"Perish thou!" he cried out.

The girl glanced at him with pain.

"Father, what is my guilt?"

"Stand here. Don't move; I will go and beg him to let us cook the potatoes only."

He went.

Shortly in the hall was heard the scuffling of feet, uplifted voices, and then Lorenz was pushed violently out on the street. He stood a moment, then said abruptly to the girl:

"Let us go."

She stooped down to gather her things. They were too heavy for her exhausted strength; but he did not help her, as if forgetting, as if not seeing that the girl could scarcely move them.

They started off. These two pitiful figures of a girl and an old man would have attracted the attention of the passers-by, had they not been accustomed to such sights of misery. Where could they go?

To what darkness, to what woe, to what
pain?

The breathing of the girl became
labored. She swayed on her feet once,
then twice, and then said, in a pleading
tone:

"Father, carry these things, I cannot
any more."

He spoke, as if awakening from a dream:

"Throw them away, then."

"Perhaps we will need them."

"We shall never need them."

Seeing that the girl hesitated, he exclaimed with rage;

"Throw them away, or I will beat you."
This time she was frightened, and obeyed
him, and they went on their way. The
peasant repeated several times:

"If so, let it be so."

Then he was silent, but a wild look
came in his eyes. They continued on
through a muddy street, which ran to the

river, passing by a building with the sign,
"Sailors' Asylum," and went upon one of
the piers, where a new dock was being
built. The large derricks of the piling
machines stood high in the air, and car-
penters were working upon scaffolding.
Mary sat down on a pile of lumber. She
was too weak to go further. Lorenz sat
silently by her side.

It was four o'clock in the afternoon.
The whole place was astir with life and
motion. The mist disappeared, and the
life-giving rays of the evening sun threw
its merciful light and warmth upon the
two sufferers. The breath of the spring
arose from the water, and the air was
brisk, full of life and gladsome. There
was so much blue and light around that
their eyes closed from its intensity. On
the background of this blue could be seen
funnels, masts. and flags waving lightly in
the breeze. The taut sails looked like

clouds in the rays of the sun, and shone
with a blinding whiteness. Steamers
sailed for distant ports, leaving a foamy
track in their wake. They were going in
the direction of Lipintse, which was for
them both a memory of lost happiness, a
better fate, and peace. Mary thought, as
she sat there: what sin have we committed
against God that He should turn his face
from us, that He, so merciful, should forsake us among a strange people on a far-off
distant shore? It was in His power to give
them back their happiness. Many vessels
went toward Lipintse, but they went without them. So the weary thoughts of the
poor girl wandered again to her old home
and to John, the hostler. Did he remember her? She remembered him, because
in happiness one may forget, but in distress and loneliness the thoughts entwine
around the beloved ones as hops around
the poplar tree. But he—perhaps he has

forsaken his old love and sent the match-
makers to another house.   It would be a
shame for him to think of such a poor
girl, who has nothing but a garland of
rue, and to whom the match-makers will
bring, as a groom, death alone.

She felt so ill that hunger did not annoy
her any more, and a feeling of drowsiness
overcame her; her eyes closed gradually and her head sank on her breast;
sometimes she opened her eyes and then
closed them again.   She dreamed that,
wandering in some ravine, she fell into
the river Danube, like Kassya in the song,
and she heard distinctly the next verse,
which describes how John, who had wit-
nessed her accident from a high cliff, de-
scended by a rope which proved to be too
short by one yard, whereupon the girl
reached up a braid of her hair and was
saved.

She suddenly awakened, for she felt in

the dream that she had no braided locks, and that she was sinking in the water. Her dream was over. Not John, but Lorenz was sitting by her side; not the blue Danube, but the docks of New York, with a forest of masts and funnels, were to be seen, and the words of a song floated to her from some passing pleasure craft. The quiet, warm, clear spring evening began to redden upon the water and sky. The surface became as smooth as a mirror; every ship and mast was reflected, as if another ship and other masts were underneath, and all was beautiful around. The air was mild and balmy; it seemed as if the whole world was glad—all but these two, who were so unhappy and forsaken; the workmen began to return home, but these two had no home.

The ever-increasing pangs of hunger tore with an iron hand at Lorenz's vitals. The peasant was sitting gloomy and downcast, but some frightful decision was expressed on his face. It had the appearance of some ravenous animal, and at the same time it had the despairing immobility of death. It was frightful to look upon. All this time he never uttered a word, but when night came and the dock was deserted, he said, with a strange voice:

" Let us go, Mary."

" Where shall we go?" she dreamily asked.

" To the end of the pier. Let us lie there and sleep."

They cautiously threaded their way along the dock to the end of the pier, fearing they might fall into the water. When they reached the edge, Lorenz said:

" Here we shall sleep."

Mary fell down on the dock, and despite the swarms of mosquitoes, she slept heavily. Suddenly in the depth of

the night the voice of Lorenz awakened
her.

"Mary, arise!"

The tone of his voice was so strange
that she awoke at once.

"What is it, father?"

In the silence and darkness of the night
the voice of the old peasant sounded hol-
low, mournful, yet quiet.

"Maiden, never more shalt thou suffer
from hunger. Thou wilt never knock at
the stranger's door to ask for bread; thou
wilt never again sleep out of doors! Man
has forsaken thee, God has forsaken thee;
thy fortune hath fled. Let death then
clasp thee to its breast. The water is
deep and thou wilt not suffer."

In the darkness she could not see him,
though her eyes were wide open from
terror.

"I will drown thee, my poor one, and
I shall drown myself," continued he;

"there is no help for us, there is no mercy for us. To-morrow thou wilt not suffer from hunger, to-morrow will be better for thee than to-day."

No! she did not want to die. She was only eighteen years of age, she had the love of life and fear of death which youth gives. Her soul shook to its depths at the thought that to-morrow she would be a corpse, that she would go into the darkness, that she would lie in the water among fishes and reptiles upon the slimy bottom. No, never! Undescribable aversion and terror enveloped her, and her own father speaking thus in the darkness seemed to her as an evil spirit.

During all this time both his hands were resting on her shoulders, and the voice continued with its dreadful, quiet insistence:

"If thou dost cry, no one will hear

thee; I will push thee, and all will not
last more than two prayers."

"No, no, father! I don't want to die,"
cried Mary. "Don't you fear God? My
dear, good father! Have mercy upon me.
What have I done to thee? I complained
not at our misfortune. I shared patiently with thee the cold and hunger.
Father!"

His breathing became short, his hands
clutched her like a vise; she begged for
her life, more and more despairingly.

"Have mercy! mercy! Am not I thy
child? I am poor, sick: I have not long
to live. I grieve; I fear to die."

Thus groaning, she clung to his coat
and imploringly pressed her lips to the
hands that tried to push her into the
water. But all this seemed to arouse him.
His quietness changed into frenzy; he
began to pant and snort; at times he made
no noise, and any one standing near

would only have heard loud breathing
and scuffling of feet on the dock. The
night was black and dark, and help there
was none; besides, it was at the far end of
the pier, and no one could hear them.

"Mercy! mercy!" screamed Mary.

At this moment he pulled her violently
with one hand on to the edge of the pier,
and with the other he beat her head to
stifle her cries. But even these cries did
not awaken an echo; only a dog howled
in the distance.

The girl felt that she was growing
weaker. Then she felt that her foot
were hanging over the edge, her hands
clung to her father, and she felt them
slipping. Her cries for help became
fainter and fainter. At last her weight
tore a piece from her father's coat, and
she was sensible that she was falling.

Unconsciously she clung to one of the
piles and hung over the water.

Lorenz stooped, and terrible to say, he began to unloosen her hands.

Crowds of thoughts like flocks of birds flew through her mind, and pictures flashed before her eyes like lightning: Lipintse, the well with its sweep, departure, the ship, the storm, the litany, New York, misery, and at last the present moment. Then she sees a great ship with uplifted bows, crowded with people, and from their midst two hands stretch out to her; thank God! it is John who stands there; he stretches forth his hands, and above the ship is the Blessed Mother, surrounded by light and smiling on her. Seeing this, she strives to come nearer: "Most Holy Virgin! John! John!" One moment more. . . . In this last moment she lifts her eyes to her father. "Father! there is the Divine Mother! there is the Divine Mother!"

One moment more, and the same hands

that had pushed her to death grasped her wrists, and with superhuman strength dragged her upon the pier. Again she feels under her feet the solid planks, again she feels arms around her, but those are the arms of a father, not of an executioner, and her head falls fainting on his breast.

On regaining her senses she saw that she was lying by the side of her father on the dock. Though it was dark, she observed that he lay with his arms outspread like a cross, and his body was convulsed with the sobs that tore his breast.

"Mary," gasped he, between his sobs, "forgive me, child!"

In the darkness the girl found his hands, and pressing her poor lips to them whispered:

"Father, may the Lord forgive thee as I forgive thee."

From a pale brightness on the horizon

emerged the moon, large, clear, and full. Again something wonderful happened. Mary saw, as in a vision, that from the moon were detached myriads of cherubim, like golden bees, which were descending to her upon the rays, their wings fluttering, and singing with childish voices:

"Martyred maiden, peace be to thee! poor bird, peace be to thee! flower of the field, patient and silent, peace be to thee!"

Thus singing above her, they waved the cups of white lilies and small silver bells, which rang out:

"Slumber to thee, maiden! slumber to thee! Slumber, sweetly sleep!"

A deep peacefulness filled her soul, and she slept.

The night was passing; it became pale— the dawn was approaching and whitened the water; the masts and funnels began to take shape; Lorenz knelt, bending over Mary.

He thought she had died. Her lithe figure was motionless; her eyes were closed; her face was as pale as wax, with a bluish tint, quiet and rigid. Vainly the old man shook her shoulder: she did not move or open her eyes. It seemed to Lorenz that she would die, but putting his hand to her mouth he felt that she still breathed. Her heart was beating, though faintly; but he thought that she would die every moment. If from the morning mist should come a clear day, if the sun would warm her, then she would come to life; if not, she would die.

The sea-gulls circled over her head, as if caring for her. The morning mists dispersed slowly before the breath of the western wind: the breath was of the spring, warm and full of sweetness.

Then the sun arose. His rays fell first on the tops of the masts, then coming lower, threw their golden light upon the entranced face of Mary. They seemed to kiss, caress, and surround her. In this light, in the halo of her beautiful hair, which had become unfastened in her struggle, she appeared angelic. By her martyrdom and misfortune, indeed Mary was now nearly an angel.

A beautiful rosy day was rising from the water; the air became warmer; the sweet breezes fanned her face; the sea-gulls hovering over her cried as if to awaken her. Lorenz took his coat and covered her feet, and hope entered his breast.

The blue tint faded from her face, her cheeks took on a healthier hue, she smiled once or twice, and at last opened her eyes.

Then the old peasant knelt on the pier, lifted his eyes to heaven, and tears rolled down his cheeks.

He felt that from now henceforward this child was the pupil of his eye, soul of his soul, holy and beloved above all.

She awoke refreshed, feeling stronger and better than yesterday. The pure air of the harbor was more healthy for her than the poisoned atmosphere of the room. She had indeed returned to life, for seated on the pier she cried out:

"Father, I am very hungry."

"Come, daughter, let us go down to the edge of the water, and perhaps we will find something there," said the old man.

She arose without much effort, and they went along the dock. It seemed as if this day was to be an exception to others, for they had only proceeded a few paces when they observed in the lumber a small bundle, which contained some bread and corn-beef. One of the workmen had only eaten part of his lunch yesterday; but Lorenz and Mary explained this more simply. Who put these victuals here? In their opinion it was He who cares for every flower, bird, grasshopper, and ant.

God!

They said their prayers, ate what they had, although it was not much, and went along the water-front to a larger dock. They felt a new strength. After resting awhile they walked for about an hour, then turned into Water Street, where they again rested on some boxes. They proceeded without knowing why, but it seemed to Mary as if she must go there. On the way they met a number of loaded wagons, and the street was alive with people. In the doorway of a business place stood a tall man with gray hair and mustache, and a young boy was by his side. He glanced at their faces and then at their dress and twirled his mustache; astonishment was depicted on his face; then he looked more closely and began to smile.

A human face, smiling friendly upon them in New York! What a miracle!

Seeing which, they were both greatly astonished.

The gentleman approached them and inquired in the purest Polish:

"Where are you from, good people?"

They felt as if lightning had struck them. The peasant, instead of answering, became pale and wavered on his feet, neither believing his ears nor eyes. Mary, who came to her senses first, knelt down at the feet of the old gentleman, embraced his knees, and began to speak:

"From Poznan, your bright highness— from Poznan."

"What are you doing here?"

"In misery, in hunger, in severe suffering we live here, dear master." Here her voice failed her; then Lorenz threw himself prone at the feet of the gentleman and began to kiss the corner of his coat, holding on to it as if he had at last found succor.

"This master is from our country. He will not let us die from hunger; he will save us; he will not let us perish."

The young boy who accompanied the gentleman looked with surprise; a crowd gathered and stared with astonishment at seeing one man kneeling before another and kissing his feet. In America this is an unusual sight. The old gentleman became impatient with the gaping crowd.

"It is none of your affair; go on about your business," he said to them in English.

Then turning to Lorenz and Mary, he said:

"Don't let us stand here—follow me."

He led them into his place of business, and taking them into a private room he shut the door.

They again began to fall down on their knees, to which he objected, muttering angrily:

"Stop that nonsense! Are we not from

the same country? Are we not children
of the same mother?"

Here, evidently, the smoke from his
cigar had got in his eyes, for wiping them
with his hand, he said:

"Are you hungry?"

"For two days we have eaten nothing,
only what little we found to-day on the
wharf."

"William," he said to the boy, "get
them something to eat." Then he inquired
further:

"Where do you live?"

"Nowhere, your highness."

"Where did you sleep?"

"On the pier."

"Did they put you out of your room?"

"They did."

"Have you nothing but what you wear?"

"We have not."

"Have you any money?"

"We have not."

"What will you do?"

"We don't know."

The old gentleman asked all these questions quickly and impatiently, and then turned suddenly to Mary and said:

"How old are you, girl?"

"I will be eighteen years old on the Ascension of our Lord."

"Have you suffered much?"

She answered nothing, but only bowed humbly.

The smoke again evidently annoyed the old gentleman.

At this moment was brought a warm meal with some beer. The old gentleman ordered them to eat at once, and when they said that they dared not do it in his presence he said they were foolish. In spite of his impatient manner he seemed to them an angel from heaven.

He enjoyed seeing them eat. Then he asked them to tell him how they came here and what they had passed through. So Lorenz told him all, keeping nothing back, as if he was telling his priest at confession. During this recital the gentleman frequently ejaculated, as if with pity, and occasionally swore mildly, and when Lorenz told of his attempt to drown Mary the old gentleman exclaimed:

"I could flay you alive for that."

Then to Mary he said:

"Come here, girl."

When she approached he took her head in both his hands and kissed her on the forehead. He thought a few moments and then said:

"You have indeed suffered. But this is a good country, only one should know how to help himself."

Lorenz opened wide his eyes. This honorable and wise gentleman called America a good country!

"It is so, you stupid!" he said, seeing

the astonishment of Lorenz—"a good country. When I came here I had nothing; now I make my living. You peasants should stay at home and till the soil, and not go traveling around. When you all leave the country what will become of it? You are not good for anything here; it is easy to come, but difficult to return."

He sat in silence for some time, and then he added, as if to himself:

"Forty years have I been in this country, and have forgotten somewhat. But a strong longing returns sometimes. William must go there—let him see where his fathers lived. This is my son," he said, pointing to the boy. "William, you will bring me a handful of soil to put under my head when I am dead?"

"Yes, father," answered the boy in English.

"And upon my breast, William—upon my breast!"

"Yes, father."

The smoke again got into the eyes of the old gentleman, so that they were suffused with tears.

Then he began to speak crossly, and said, pointing to the boy:

"This dude understands Polish, but he prefers to speak English. But it can't be helped. The people who come here are lost to the old country. William, go and tell your sister that we shall have guests for dinner and for the night."

The boy went quickly. The old gentleman fell into a reverie and was silent for some time; then he began to speak, as if to himself:

"If I send them back it will cost considerable, and what will they return to?" They have sold what they had; they will become paupers. If the girl goes out as a servant, what will become of her? Now they are here it is better that I find them

work. The best way is to send them to
some agricultural colony out West; there
they can settle. The girl will marry
there; they will accumulate some money,
and if they wish to return they can take
back the old man."

Turning to Lorenz he said:

"Did you learn anything about Polish
settlements in America?"

"I did not, your highness."

"My dear people, how did you come
here without understanding anything?
For the Lord's sake! it is no wonder that
you came near perishing. In Chicago
there are twenty thousand such as you—
in Milwaukee just as many, in Detroit
quite a number, and in Buffalo also.
They all work in factories; but for the
peasants it is better for them to be on a
farm. I would send you to Radom, Illinois, to the Polish settlement there, but the
land is all taken up. They have founded

a new city of Poznan on the Nebraska prairies, but it is too far; the railroad fare is too much. The 'Virgin Mary' colony, in Texas, is also too far. The best place to send you is to Borowina, especially as I can get you passes, and what money I give you you can then save for your new home."

He again fell into a reverie.

"Listen, old man," said he suddenly. "They are founding a new colony, called Borowina, in Arkansas. It is a beautiful country, and warm, and the land is not yet taken up. There you can get land together with woods, one hundred and sixty acres, from the government free, or from the railroad for a small payment. Do you understand? I will get you tickets and give you some money to start farming with. You will go on the cars to Little Rock and thence by wagon. Besides, I will give you letters of introduction. I

want to help you, because I am your
brother; and especially I pity your daughter. Do you understand? You should
thank God that you met me."

Here his voice became mild.

"Listen, child," he said to Mary, "here
is my card; keep it carefully. If some
misfortune happen to thee, if thou art
left alone in the world and without protection, then come to me. Thou art a
poor child and good. If I should die
William will take care of you. Don't lose
the card. Now let us go to my house."

Upon the way he purchased some clean
linen and clothing for them, and after-
ward he brought them to his house and
treated them as guests. Every one was
very kind to them. William and his sister
Jenny used them as if they were relatives.
Master William addressed Mary as if she
was a lady, which confused her very
much. In the evening several nicely

dressed young ladies came to call on
Jenny. They were very much interested in
Mary and made friends with her at once;
they wondered at her paleness, her beauty,
her bright hair, and when she kissed their
hands they laughed heartily. The old
gentleman took part in their conversation,
shook his white head, muttered, and sometimes pretended to be angry; he spoke
sometimes in English and sometimes in
Polish; discussed with Lorenz and Mary
about the old country; tried to recall
places, mused, and from time to time,
being again annoyed by the smoke of his
cigar, would wipe his eyes.

When it came time for them to go to
rest, Mary could not withhold her tears on
seeing Miss Jenny preparing her bed for
her. Ah! what good people these are!
But no wonder. Was not the old gentleman also from Poznan?

On the third day Lorenz and Mary were

on their way to Little Rock.   The peasant
had one hundred dollars in his pocket and
had entirely forgotten his sufferings.
Mary felt that above her was the guiding
hand of God, and trusted that He would
not let her perish: that as He had brought
her out of misfortune, He would lead John
to America, take care of them both, and
guide them back to Lipintse.

Meanwhile, cities, villages and farms
flashed by their car window. It was entirely different from New York. There were
fields and pastures and forests in the far distance, and houses shaded by trees, and immense stretches of young green crops were
everywhere, just as in Poland. At this sight
Lorenz felt his bosom fill with gladness,
so that he had a desire to cry out: "I
greet thee, forests and green fields!"
Upon the meadows were pastured herds of
cows and flocks of sheep; at the edge of
the woods could be seen men cutting the

trees down with axes. The train flew
farther and farther; the country was getting less and less settled. Farms disappeared, and in their place could be seen
the wide, open prairies. The wind swayed
waves of grass and flowers. Strips of yellow flowers covered the plains in spots,
winding like golden ribbons. The high
grass, mulleins, and thistles bent their
heads as if greeting the travelers. Hawks
hovered over the plains on their wide
wings watching for their prey. The train
rushed forward as if wishing to reach the
point where the prairies merged into the
horizon. From the window of the car
could be occasionally seen jack rabbits and
towns of prairie dogs. Sometimes the
antlers of the kingly elk would rise from
the brakes. Nowhere could be seen a
church steeple, city, village, house—nothing but the lonely railway station. Lorenz

looked at all this, and he could not understand why so much good land lay idle.

A day and night passed. The next
morning the train entered deep woods
where the trees were entwined with vines
as thick as a human arm, which circum-
stance made the forest so dense that you
would be compelled to cut your way
through with an ax. Unknown birds sang
in these great thickets. Once it appeared
to Lorenz and Mary that they saw some
riders with feathers in their hair and faces
as red as polished brass. Seeing these
woods, these deserted plains and forests,
and these strange wild kind of people, and
all these wonders, Lorenz could not stand
it any longer and said:

"Mary."

" What is it, father?"

"Do you see?"

" Yes, I do."

"And do you marvel?"

"Yes, I do marvel."

At last they crossed a mighty river, which was three times wider than the Warta, and which, they found out later, was the Mississippi, and in the middle of the night they came to Little Rock.

From here they had to inquire their way to Borowina.

We will leave them for a moment. The second period in their search for bread is ended. The third will be in the woods, resounding with axes, and in the hardships and toil of pioneer life. If there were in it less tears, suffering and ill-fate, we shall shortly know.

CHAPTER III.

PIONEER LIFE.

WHAT was Borowina? It was a projected settlement not yet in existence.
The name was first invented, conforming
to the rule that where there is a name
there must be a place. The Polish and
even American newspapers published in
New York, Chicago, Buffalo, Detroit,
Milwaukee, Denver, in a word, in every
place where the Polish language could
be heard, proclaimed *urbi et orbi* generally, and to Polish circles particularly.
that if any one wished to be healthy,
rich, happy, to live on the fat of the land,
to live long and to have sure salvation
after death, he should buy a farm in the
earthly paradise of Borowina. These an-

nouncements said that Arkansas, in which stood Borowina, was as yet unsettled, but the most salubrious place in the world. Truly the city of Memphis, which lies opposite Arkansas, on the other side of the Mississippi, was the home of the yellow fever; yet, according to the advertisements, neither yellow nor any other kind of fever could cross so wide a river as the Mississippi. They have a saying that on the high banks of the Arkansas River the yellow fever never appears, because the Choctaw Indians of that neighborhood would scalp it without pity. Therefore fever trembles at the sight of a redskin. As a result of this state of affairs, the settlers of Borowina would live between the fever on the east and the redskins on the west, in an entirely neutral belt; therefore, having such a grand future before it, Borowina in a thousand years undoubtedly would have two millions of inhabitants, and the

ground, which now costs a dollar and fifty
cents an acre, would then be worth a thousand dollars a square yard.

It was difficult to resist these allure-
ments. For those who disliked the close
proximity of the Choctaws, the announce-
ments assured them that this bellicose
tribe had a particular affection for Poles,
so that nothing but the most pleasant
relations could be foreseen. Besides, it
was asserted that where a railroad and
telegraph poles, in the shape of crosses,
passed through the country, these crosses
would all soon be monuments for the
graves of Indians; and as the land of Borowina was purchased from the railroad,
the disappearance of the Indians was then
only a question of time.

The land was indeed bought from the
railroad, which assured to the settlement
connection with the world, a market for
their produce, and argued well for its

future development.   These advertisements neglected to add that this railroad
was only a projected one, and that the
proceeds of the sales of the quarter sections
of land, given by the government to the
railroad, were necessary to complete the
fund for its building; but this forgetfulness must be forgiven in so complicated a
business.   The only difference to Borowina was that the settlement, instead of
being on a line of a railroad, was out in
the wilderness and could only with great
difficulty be reached by wagon.

From this forgetfulness might arise different misunderstandings, but they were
temporary and would disappear with the
building of the road.   Besides, it was
known that the advertisements in this
country were not taken literally, because,
as every shrub transplanted in American
soil grows luxuriantly at the expense of its
fruit. so also advertisements in American

papers grow so large and resplendent that
it is difficult to thresh out the grain of
truth from the rhetorical chaff.   Yet, setting aside all in these advertisements that
was *humbug*, it might be admitted that this
settlement was not worse than thousands
of others whose beginning was announced
with a similar grandiloquence.

The conditions seemed to be, from many
standpoints, quite fortunate, and quite a
number of Polish persons and even families, scattered throughout the States, from
the Great Lakes to the palm groves of
Florida, from the Atlantic to the California
coast, subscribed as settlers to this colony.
The Mazurs from Prussia, the Silesians,
the people from Poznan, the Galicians,
the Lithuanians from Augustow, and Mazurs from Warsaw, who were working in
the factories in Chicago and Milwaukee,
who longed for a life which a peasant, the
son of a peasant, ought to lead, grasped at

the first chance to get themselves out of
the stifling, smoky cities, to take up a
plow and an ax on the broad prairies,
fields, and woods of Arkansas. Those for
whom Texas was too warm, or Minnesota
too cold, or Michigan too damp, or Illinois
too crowded, joined with the first ones,
and several hundred people, composed
mostly of men, but with quite a number
of women and children, started for Arkansas. The different tales they heard did
not deter them. Indeed, this section
abounds with bloodthirsty Indians, out-
laws, frontiersmen, and adventurers, and
the western part of the State is famous for
its encounters between the Indian and
white hunters and the frequent lynchings
that take place. The settlers thought
that in the course of time this lawlessness
would die out. A Mazur, when he has a
club in his hand, and especially when he
has other Mazurs at his back, will not be

driven from his path, and to those who
would molest him he is ready to exclaim:
"Have a care; we are not fools; dare not
to touch us, or we will lame you." It is
known that the Mazurs like to band together, to settle in bodies, so that one can
run with his club in his hand to help
another.

The gathering point for the majority
was the city of Little Rock, but from there
to Clarksville, the nearest settlement to
Borowina, was farther than from Warsaw
to Cracow, and what was worse, their way
lay across an unsettled country, heavy
woods, and swollen rivers. A few who
had started out alone got lost in the woods
and perished, but the main body of the
emigrants had proceeded safely on their
way and were now camping in the woods,
having reached their destination. After
they had arrived on the ground they were
greatly disappointed; they had expected

to get prairie land, interspersed with
woods, but they found only a forest, which
they must clear. The black oaks, the
redwood, the cottonwood, the bright plat-
anes, the gloomy hickories, all stood in
one mass. This was no forest to laugh at.
It had a thick growth of chaparral underneath, and above the branches of the trees
were interlaced, like network, and to them
clung vines, which, hanging in heavy
strands from tree to tree, looked like sus-
pension bridges, like festoons, like immense garlands, covered with flowers. So
thick, dense, and impenetrable were they
that the eye could not see afar off, like in
the northern woods; he who ventured
there could not see the sky above his head,
was compelled to walk in the dark, and
would be lost therein. The Mazurs looked
first at their hands, then at their axes,
then at the trees, several yards in circum-
ference, and felt discouraged. It is well

to have wood with which to build houses and for fires, but for one man to cut down a forest of one hundred and sixty acres, to tear the stumps out of the ground, to level the soil and then to plow it, is the labor of years.

But they had no choice. On the second day after their arrival each man crossed himself, breathed upon the palms of his hands, grasped his ax, swung and struck, and from that time every day was heard the ringing of axes in this Arkansas forest, and sometimes they resounded with the echo of songs.

Their camp was pitched in a large glade, near the edge of a stream. They intended on this glade to build a city in the form of a square, with a church and schoolhouse in the center. All that was for the future; and in its place stood the emigrant wagons which had brought their families and household goods. The wagons were cor-

raled in a triangular form, so that they
would form a fortress in case of attack.
Outside the wagons, on the rest of this
glade, grazed mules, horses, and cattle,
which were guarded by young lads who
were armed. The women slept in the
wagons and the men around the fires.

In the daytime the women and children
stayed in the camp; the near presence of
the men could be known by the sound of
the axes, which rang all over the woods.
At night could be heard the cries of wild
animals in the woods—pumas, wolves, and
coyotes; the frightful gray bears, which
the light of the fires did not scare, approached the wagons quite closely, and
then could be heard the report of rifles
and the cry, "Come and help us to kill
the beast." They who came from the
wilds of Texas were mostly skilled hunters
and supplied the camp with game—deer,
elk, and antelope; it was the time of the

spring migration of these animals to the north. They had also a supply of provisions, bought in Little Rock and Clarksville, consisting of flour, corn meal, and salt pork; besides, they occasionally killed a sheep, having brought a large number with them. In the evening, when a great fire was started near the wagons after supper, the young people would dance instead of going to sleep. Some one had brought a violin with him, on which he played. The first thing was to build the houses, and soon, indeed, upon the green turf could be seen a number in process of erection; nearly all the surface of the glade was covered with shavings, chips, and pieces of bark. The redwood could be quite easily worked, but often it was necessary to go quite a distance to get it. Some constructed for themselves temporary tents out of the canvas coverings of the wagons. Others, especially the un-

married men, who did not care to have
a roof over their heads so soon, and who
did not like the work of woodchopping,
began to plow in spots where there was no
undergrowth and where the oaks and hickories were farther apart. Then for the
first time in the Arkansas woods were
heard the cries, " Gee! haw! g'lang!"

Indeed, there was so much work for the
settlers to do that it was difficult for them
to decide what to do first—to build houses,
clear some land, or hunt game. It seemed
that the projectors of this colony bought
the land from the railroad company on
faith, without having first examined it.
Otherwise they would never have selected
such thick woods, while it would have
been just as easy for them to have pro-
cured prairie lands, only partially covered
with trees. One of the leading spirits of
this enterprise and a railroad official appeared on the scene to survey the land and

make the allotments, but seeing the true
state of affairs, spent only two days there,
and after a violent quarrel they left, saying they were going to Clarksville for
surveying tools, but never returned.

Soon it came out that some settlers paid
more and some less, and what was worse,
no one knew where his lot lay, or even
how to survey it, if they could locate it.
They were without guidance, power to
order their affairs, or smooth their misunderstandings. They had not the experi-
ence to know how to go to work.

A body of Germans would have com-
bined together to clear the woods, build
houses, and then would have measured off
to each man his portion; but the Mazur,
at the beginning, wanted to settle on his
own land, to build his own house, and to
cut down trees on his own lot. Every one
wanted also to get land near the central
glade, where the trees were few and water

the nearest. Thereupon arose contentions,
which gradually grew, when on a certain
day there appeared, as if falling from
heaven, the wagon of a Mr. Grunmanski.
In Cincinnati, where he came from, he
was called Mr. Grunman, but in Borowina
he added the "ski" to his name to obtain
favor in the eyes of the Poles. His wagon
had a high canvas covering, upon each
side of which there was painted the word
"Saloon" in large black letters, and under
that in smaller letters, "Brandy, whiskey,
gin." How this wagon made the danger-
ous trip alone between Clarksville and
Borowina, without being robbed by the
desperadoes or Mr. Gruumanski getting
scalped by the Indians, was a mystery; it
is enough to know that he did arrive, and
from the first day began to do a good business. On that selfsame day the settlers
began to quarrel. The thousand disputes
about land, tools, sheep, places at the fire,

were now augmented and embittered by
the slightest causes. In the minds of the
settlers was awakened some silly American
provincialisms. Those who came from
the Northern States began to compare and
extol their old homes above those of the
Southern States, and *vice versa*. Then
could be heard a mixture of Polish and
American slang.

Affairs went very badly in the settlement now. for the people were like a flock
of sheep without a shepherd. The quarrels about the land became more and more
violent. Fights arose where the associates
from one city or place joined against those
from another section. Those who were
more experienced, old and wise, gradually
acquired some authority and influence, but
they could not always maintain order.
The common instinct of self-preservation
in times of danger compelled them to forget
their quarrels for the time being. Once,

when a band of renegade Indians drove off
a herd of sheep, the settlers banded quickly together and went in pursuit of them;
they recovered their sheep and one Indian
was killed and harmony prevailed all that
day, but next morning they again commenced fighting among themselves. Harmony reigned in the evenings, when the
musician played, not dances, but the different songs that they had all sung long
ago in their cottages at home. Talk then
ceased. The settlers gathered around the
musician in a great circle, the murmur of
the forest accompanied him, the camp-
fires hissed and sparkled, the listeners
bowed their heads and their sad souls flew
beyond the sea. Sometimes the moon
rose high above the forest, and they still
listened. But with the exception of these
short, quiet intervals, everything was becoming disrupted and disorganized in the
community. Disorder grew and hatred

began. This little commonwealth, strand-
ed in these woods, isolated from the rest
of the world, abandoned by its guides and
protectors, could not and did not know
how to help itself.

Among these settlers we now find our
two old friends, Lorenz Toporek and his
daughter Mary. Having got to Arkansas,
they had to share in Borowina the lot of
others. At the beginning it was not so
bad for them. The forest was not the
hard pavements of New York; there they
had nothing, while here they possessed a
wagon, some provisions and tools bought
in Clarksville. There the frightful longing continually gnawed them; here the
hard work kept their minds busy. The
peasant cut down trees from morning to
night, squared the timbers with his ax and
put them together; the girl washed their
clothes in the creek, made the fire and
cooked their meals; the exercise and open

air of the woods gradually destroyed on
her face all traces of her illness and suffering in New York. The hot breezes
tanned and covered her pale face with a
golden hue. The young boys from San
Antonio, who were always ready to fight
on the slightest provocation with the
youths from the Great Lakes, all agreed
on this one thing: that Mary's eyes looked
from under her bright hair as blue as the
cornbottle flower amid the golden rye, and
that she was the most beautiful maiden
ever seen by human eye. Mary's beauty
was of some use to Lorenz. He selected a
good piece of woods and no one objected,
because all the young men favored his
claim. They helped him also to fell the
trees, square the timbers and build his
house, and the old man, understanding
their reasons, would say to them from
time to time:

"My daughter walks upon the mead-

ows like a lily, like a lady, like a princess.
I can give her to him whom I like, but it
is not every one who will get her, because
she is the daughter of a landowner. The
one who will bow lowest to me and be
respectful to me, he may get her, but no
ne'er-do-well will ever get her."

Those then who helped him thought
that thereby they would gain favor in his
eyes.

So Lorenz felt better than the others,
and he would have been all right if the settlement had any future before it. But mat-
ters were getting worse day by day. One
week passed, then another. Quite a clearing was made, the earth was covered with
chips, here and there arose the walls of
the yellow log houses; but that which was
accomplished was a mere bagatelle to that
which ought to be done. The green walls
of the forest receded very slowly before
the attack of the axes. Those who made

some explorations brought the news that
the forest was without end, that there
were frightful swamps and bayous and
stagnant water under the trees, that some
monsters dwelt there, and misty, ghostlike
forms floated among the trees, that it was
alive with hissing snakes, and weird voices
cried, "Keep away." A young man from
Chicago asserted that he saw the very devil
himself, who lifted his shaggy head with
flaming eyes out of the swamp and snorted
at him, on which he fled. The settlers
from Texas explained to him that it must
have been a buffalo, but he would not be-
lieve them. These superstitious stories
increased the unpleasantness of the threatening situation. Several days after the
devil had been seen it happened that two
of the young men went into the woods and
were never seen again. A number of the
men were now stricken with chills and
fever. The quarrels about the division

of land became so bitter that they often
led to blows and severe bodily injuries.
Those who did not brand their cattle were
denied ownership in them by others. The
corral was broken up, and the wagons
were scattered in all corners of the clearing, so as to be further off from each
other. They could not agree as to who
would guard the stock and the sheep
were getting lost.

One thing became evident, that before
they could grow any grain their provisions
would be exhausted and starvation would
threaten them. They began to despair.
The ring of the ax in the woods grew less
frequent because they were losing their
patience and courage. Everybody would
have been willing to work hard if they
could have been assured as to their own
property. But no one knew what was his
and what was not. The complaints grew
louder on all sides. They said they had

been led out into the wilderness to perish.
Those who had any money left took their
wagons and started, one by one, for Clarksville.   But the majority, having spent all
their money in this enterprise, were compelled to remain.   Seeing nothing but
ruin before them in their extremity, they
wrung their hands.   At last the axes
ceased entirely and the forest laughed as
if with glee at the insignificance of human
efforts. "Chop! chop! for two years and
then die of starvation," said they to each
other.   And the forest answered as if
mocking.   One evening Lorenz came to
Mary and said:

"I see that all will perish here, and we
shall perish also."

"If it is God's will," answered the girl.
"He was merciful before to us, and even
now He will not forsake us."

As she spoke she raised her blue eyes to
the stars, and by the light of the fire she

looked like a picture of a saint, and the young men, looking at her, said:

"And we shall not forsake you, Mary, for you are as beautiful as the morning dawn to us."

She thought to herself that there was only one with whom she would go to the end of the world—her John—John in Lipintse. But he, who had promised to swim to her over the sea like a duck, to fly to her like a falcon through the air, to roll like a golden hoop on the road, he swam not, flew not, and above all others was not with her—she was alone, the poor one.

Mary could but know that all was not well in the settlement, for she had already been in dire straits. God had saved her from the deep abysses, her soul had become radiant through suffering, so that nothing could now shake her faith in the help of heaven. She remembered also the

good old gentleman in New York who had
rescued them from their misery and had
helped them to come here—had given her
his card and told her if she was ever in
trouble to come to him and he would take
care of her.

Meanwhile the settlement was threatened more and more every day. Men deserted in the night-time and what befell
them it was difficult to say; while around
the forest still mocked.

Old Lorenz at last fell sick. The pain
racked his spine. For two days he neglected it and the third day he could not
get up from his bed. The girl went to
the woods, gathered some moss, spread
it on a platform made of logs, made a
comfortable bed for her father, and cooked
some herbs and roots as medicine for him.

"Mary," muttered the old man, "I
feel that death is coming for me through
the woods; thou wilt be an orphan, alone

in the world. God now punishes me for
my heavy sins, for I led thee over the seas
to perdition. Hard it will be for me to
die."

"Father," answered the girl, "God
would have punished me if I had not come
with thee over the seas."

"If it were not for leaving thee alone,
if I could only bless thy marriage, it
would be easier for me to die. Take thou
Czarny Orlik for thy husband; he is a
good man—he will take care of thee."

Czarny Orlik, who was nicknamed
"Black Eagle," a famous hunter from
Texas, overheard this and at once knelt
down before the old man.

"Father, bless us!" said he; "I love
this maiden as my own life; I know the
forest well, and shall not let her perish."

Saying this, he looked at Mary with ad-
miration, but she, kneeling at the feet of
the old man, said:

"Don't ask me, father! to him whom I pledged my troth, his only shall I be."

"He to whom thou hast pledged thy troth, his thou shalt never be, for I shall slay him. Mine only must thou be," answered Orlik. "All will perish here, and thou too will perish if I do not save thee."

He was not mistaken. The settlement was dwindling. One week drifted into another. The provisions were getting low. They began to kill the working cattle. The fever claimed new victims. The people began to lament and cry to heaven for help.

One Sunday, the old and young men, women and children all knelt on the turf, and raising their voices intoned the supplication: "Holy God! Holy Mighty, Holy Immortal, have mercy upon us!" The forest stopped its swaying and murmuring and listened. When the prayer had ceased, again it deeply muttered, as if threatening: "Here I am king, here I am lord, here I am the mightiest."

"Black Eagle," who knew the forest well, looked at it fearlessly with his dark eyes and loudly said:

"I dare you! I defy you!"

One after another they all looked at Orlik and some hope entered their hearts. Those who had known him in Texas had great confidence in him, for he was famed as a hunter there. He was a youth who had been raised on the plains and was as strong as an ox. Often he went alone to kill bears. In San Antonio, where he formerly lived, they all knew that sometimes he would take his gun and be absent in the woods for several months, and always returned healthy and unharmed. They called him "Black Eagle" because he was bronzed by the sun. They said he had been a desperado on the Mexican line, but that was not true. He only brought home skins, and sometimes an Indian scalp, until the local priest threatened to excommunicate him for that. In Borowina he neither cared for nor feared anything. The forest supplied him with food and clothing. When the people became frightened and lost their heads he became the leader, having all his Texas friends to support him. After their prayers, when he showed his anger by defying the forest, they thought he would devise something.

The sun was setting; high between the black branches of the hickory was seen the golden haze; it reddened, deepened, and went out. A southerly evening breeze came up. Orlik took his rifle and went to the woods.

The night had fallen, when in the distance of the dark woods the people saw what appeared to them as a great golden star, like the dawn with the rising sun; it grew with terrible quickness, spreading out a glow as red as blood.

"The forest is on fire! the forest is on fire!" arose the cries from the camp.

Clouds of frightened birds flew out from all sides of the woods, twittering, cawing and crying. The stock began to bellow deeply, dogs howled, terrified men ran here and there, fearing they would be caught in the flames; but the strong southerly breeze could but carry the fire from the glade. Meanwhile, in the distance shone a second red star, then a third; both soon joined the first, and the blaze, now covering a great space, roared, hissed, and gained in volume. The flames poured as water, ran along the dry network of vines and shriveled up the leaves. The burning branches, carried by the wind, flew like fiery birds.

The hickories exploded with a report like cannon. The red snakes of fire

writhed on the resinous carpet of pine-
needles. The hissing, the noise, the
crackling of branches, the dull roar of the
flames, mixed with the cries of the birds
and the howls of wild animals that filled
the air. The tall trees, piercing the sky,
wavered like fiery pillars and columns.
The long, blazing vine-strands, burned
away from one end, swung with a mighty
sweep, like the tentacles of some fierce
flaming dragon, carrying sparks and fire
from tree to tree. The heavens reddened
as if itself aflame. It became as light as
day. Then the flames united in one sea
of fire and swept through the forest,
breathing death and destruction in its
pathway, like the wrath of God.

Smoke, heat, and the smell of burning
wood, filled the air. Although no danger
threatened them, the people of the camp
were alarmed and cried out and called to
each other; when suddenly from the side

of the fire, amid its sparks and glow, appeared the figure of "Black Eagle." His
face was blackened by the smoke and
looked austere. When they surrounded
him in a circle, leaning on his rifle, he
said:

"Your clearing is done. It was I who
burned the forest in that direction. To-
morrow you will have as much cleared land
as you desire." Then approaching Mary,
he said:

"Thou must be mine, for I am he who
burned the forest. Who is here more
mighty?"

The girl trembled, because the reflection of the fire blazed in the eyes of Orlik,
and he appeared to her as something terrible.

For the first time since her arrival she
thanked God that John was far away in
Lipintse.

In the meantime the roaring conflagra-

tion had receded further and further. The
dawn came, cloudy and threatening rain.
At daybreak a party started to explore the
burned regions, but they were driven back
by the intense heat. On the second day
the smoke hung in such heavy banks of
mist that nothing could be discerned a
few paces off. In the night it began rain-
ing, which soon changed into a frightful
downpour. Perhaps the forest fires had
disturbed the atmosphere and precipitated
the moisture from the clouds, or perhaps
it was the usual time, when on the Mississippi and also at the forks of the Arkansas
and Red Rivers, heavy rains begin to fall.
This is increased by the evaporation of
water, which in Arkansas covers a large
territory in the form of swamps, creeks,
and small lakes, being fed in the spring-
time by the melting snows of the far-dis-
tant mountains. The ground softened
and the glade looked like a great pond.

The dampness and exposure caused a great
deal of sickness. Some hurried away, desiring to reach Clarksville, but they soon
returned, bringing the news that the river
was so swollen with the rains that it was
impossible to ford it. The situation became alarming, because the supply of
provisions was nearly exhaused and it was
impossible to replenish them from Clarksville. Starvation threatened Lorenz and
Mary the least, for the mighty hand of
"Black Eagle" protected them. Every
morning he brought game to them, which
he had shot or caught in his traps; over
the platform where the old man lay, Orlik
had erected his tent to protect them from
the rain. From their helplessness it was
necessary for them to accept the attentions
which he forced on them and to express
their gratitude. The old man knew that
the only recompense he expected was the
hand of Mary.

"I am not the only one in the world," Mary pleadingly would say. "Go thou and find another as I love another."

But Orlik would answer:

"If I go to the end of the world I could not find another like thee. Thou art the only one in the world for me and must be mine. What wilt thou do when the old man dies? Thou wilt thyself come to me, and I will take thee as the wolf carries the lamb into the woods, but I will not eat thee. Thou art mine and mine alone. Who will deny thee to me? Of whom am I here afraid? Let thy John come—I wish it!"

As far as Lorenz was concerned Orlik seemed to be right. The old man was sinking fast; he became delirious at times, spoke of his sins, of Lipintse, and that God would never let him see it again. Mary wept over him and thought of herself. The offer of Orlik to go with her to Li-

pintse, if she would promise to be his, was
to her bitterness and wormwood. To
return to Lipintse, where John was, betrothed to another, never! Better to die
here under the trees. Such, she thought,
would be her end.

Another trial was about to fall on the
settlement.

The downpour of rain increased from
day to day. On a certain dark night,
when Orlik went as usual to the woods, in
the camp was heard a piercing shriek:
"Water! water!"

The startled settlers rising from their
sleep saw, as far as the eye could reach in
the darkness, one wide plain, splashing
under the rain and swayed by the wind.
The dimly diffused light of the night covered with its steely hue the undulating
folds and wrinkles of its waves. From
that portion of the forest which had been
devastated by the fire could be heard the

dashing and splashing of the advancing
flood. The cries of the people arose in
all directions. The women and children
began to climb into the wagons. Some of
the men ran to the western side of the
woods looking for places of safety. The
water reached to their knees and was rap-
idly rising. The noises from the woods
increased and mingled with the cries of
terror, the calling of names and the plead-
ings for help. Soon the stock stampeded
before the onslaught of the water, and it
was observed that the violence of the current increased. The sheep were carried
away, piteously bleating for help, till they
disappeared in the darkness. The rain
continued to fall in torrents, and every
moment the situation became more crit-
ical. The distant noises changed into the
mad uproar and turmoil of the waves.
The wagons began to shake and tremble
before the pressure of the water. It was

clear that this was no ordinary freshet, but that the Arkansas and all its tributaries must have overflowed their banks. The flood was tearing the trees up by the roots, breaking down the forests—terror, warring of elements, darkness, death!

One of the wagons which stood nearest to the burned woods was upset. Upon hearing the shrieks of the women for help several dark figures of men started from the trees to their assistance, but the water caught them in its embrace and whirled them into the trees and to destruction. They climbed on the roofs of the other wagons. The rain still fell in torrents, and darkness like a heavy pall enveloped everything.

Sometimes there would pass a log of timber swaying up and down, with a human figure clinging to it; and sometimes the dark form of an animal or man, sometimes an arm, would protrude from the water in one last despairing effort and disappear forever.

The hoarse, fierce noise of the waves swallowed up every other sound; the roars of the drowning animals, and the cries, "Jesus! Jesus! save us." The glade was transformed into a whirling vortex of seething water; the wagons were fast disappearing.

Where were Lorenz and Mary? The strong platform of logs, upon which the old man lay under Black Eagle's tent, for the present saved them, for it floated like a raft. The water swept it around the glade and carried it into the woods, where, after dashing against the trees, it at last emerged into the swift current of the stream and was borne away in the darkness.

The girl, kneeling by her father, lifted her hands in prayer to heaven, calling for help; but her only answer was the dashing of the wet spray on her face and the moaning of the night wind.

The tent was torn away.

Every moment the raft was threatened with destruction by the floating trees, logs and stumps which might either crush or upset it.

At last it stuck in the branches of a large uprooted tree. From one of the branches came the sound of a human voice:

"Take my rifle and move to the other side of the raft, so that it will not upset when I jump."

As soon as Mary obeyed these instructions a dark figure jumped from the branches to the raft.

It was "Black Eagle."

"Mary," said he, "as I told thee, I shall not desert thee. As God is my witness, I shall lead thee out of this gulf."

With the hatchet he had in his hunting-belt he cut a straight branch from the tree, and in a few moments fashioned a pole out of it, then pushed the raft out from the branches and began to guide it down the stream.

Having reached the middle of the current, they went with great rapidity—where they did not know, but on and on they went. Orlik from time to time pushed off the threatening logs and stumps and steered the raft clear of standing trees. His immense strength seemed to increase. His eyes, despite the darkness, discovered every danger. Hour after hour passed. Any ordinary man would have sunk under this strain, but on him were left no traces of fatigue. At dawn they left the forest behind; not the top of a tree could be seen. The whole country looked like one vast sea. A monstrous body of yellow and foamy water covered the wide prairies. The daylight grew. Orlik, seeing that

there was no stump near them, ceased his
watch for a moment and, turning toward
Mary, said:

"Now thou art surely mine, for I have
snatched thee from death."

His head was bare, his face flushed with
exercise, and, warmed with his battle with
the flood, had such an expression of power
that for the first time Mary did not dare
to answer that she was betrothed to another.

"Mary"—said the young man softly—
"dear Mary."

"Where are we floating to?" she asked,
desiring to change the subject.

"What do I care, as long as I am with
thee, dear?"

"Steer, for still death does threaten us."

Orlik began to steer again. Poor old
Lorenz felt worse and worse; at times the
fever burned him and again it left him,
but he was growing weaker. These sufferings were too much for his poor old

worn-out body. The end was approaching—a great peace, eternal relief. At noon he awoke and said:

"Mary, I shall never see to-morrow. Oh, my dear one! Oh, that I had never left Lipintse and brought thee with me! But God is merciful! Not a little have I suffered, and He will forgive me my sins. Bury me, if you can, and let Orlik bring thee to the old gentleman in New York. He is a good man and will have pity on thee and help thee to return to Lipintse. I shall never return. Oh, God! merciful and just, let my soul fly there, if but for one look."

Here he became delirious and began to mutter: "Unto thy refuge I flee, Holy Mother of God!" Then he cried out: "Don't throw me into the water; I am no dog." Then he apparently recalled his attempt on Mary's life, for he cried out: "Child, forgive me, forgive me!"

The poor thing was seated at his head weeping. Orlik steered, and tears were also in his eyes.

Toward evening the sky became clear. The setting sun showed itself above the flooded country and was reflected in the water like a long golden pathway. The old man was dying. God had mercy upon him and brought him death in the bright sunshine. First, he said, in a mournful voice: " I wandered far away from Poland, from my native land." And then, in his delirium, it seems to him that he returns to it. Lo! he now sees that the old gentleman in New York has given him money for a ticket and has repurchased his old home for him, so that Mary and he are now going back. They are upon the ocean, the ship sails day and night, and the sailors sing. Then he sees the docks of Hamburg from which he left; he passes by different cities; he hears the sound of

German speech, and the train flies onward,
so that Lorenz feels that he is nearing his
old home once more. Some joy inflates
his breast; sweet breezes are wafted to him
from his native land. What is it? He
reaches the frontier. The poor peasant's
heart beats like a trip-hammer. Hasten!
hasten! Lord! Lord! Here are now our
fields with the wild pear-trees dividing
them. Here are the gray-thatched cottages and the churches. There a peasant
in his lambskin cap, walking behind his
plow. He stretches out his hands to him
from the windows of the car. He calls
him: "Brother, brother." He can say no
more. The train speeds on. What is
this? The city of Przyremble; Lipintse is
near. Mary and he walk along the road
with tears of joy streaming down their
faces. It is spring. All is in bloom . . .
the May beetles drone in the air . . . in
Przyremble the Angelus rings out . . .

Jesus, why givest Thou so much happiness to this poor sinner? One more hill to pass; there is the cross, the signpost, and the township line of Lipintse. They do not walk now—they fly as if on wings—they are upon the hill, by the cross, by the signpost. The peasant casts himself upon the ground, weeps for very joy, kisses the soil, and crawling on his knees to the cross, throws his arms around it: he is now in Lipintse! Truly this is so. He is now in Lipintse! for only his dead body lies on this strayed raft, on the face of the desolate waters, and his soul has flown where it has at last found happiness, rest, peace.

Vainly the girl laments and cries: "Father! father!" Poor Mary, he will not return to thee! It is well for him in Lipintse!

The night fell. The pole was slipping from Orlik's hands and hunger gnawed him. Mary, kneeling over the dead body of her father, prayed as she sobbed quietly to herself, and as far as the eye could reach naught could be seen but the vast expanse of water.

They now struck the swift current of some mighty river, which carried them forward quickly. It was impossible to steer the raft; sometimes it got into a vortex and was whirled round and round. Orlik felt that his strength was leaving him, when suddenly he jumped up and cried out:

"By all the saints! I see a light."

Mary looked in the direction to which he pointed and saw a small light, which was reflected upon the water.

"It is a boat from Clarksville," quickly said Orlik. "They are a rescuing party; I hope they will not pass us. Mary, I will save thee." And then he began to shout: "Halloo! halloo!"

Simultaneously he began to steer and row frantically. The light grew larger, and in its glow the outlines of a large boat could be seen. It was still far off but was gradually approaching. After some time Orlik observed that they were drifting further apart.

They had entered some unknown current that carried them out of the pathway of the boat and were now receding from it.

Suddenly the pole broke from the great pressure put on it by Orlik.

They were now helpless. The current carried them further away and the light was diminishing. Fortunately a few minutes later the raft stuck in the branches of a tree that was standing alone on the prairie.

They both began to cry for help, but the noise of the current drowned their voices.

"I shall fire off my rifle," said Orlik;
"they will see its flash and hear the report."

As soon as he said so he raised his rifle
to his shoulder, but in place of its loud
report was heard only the click of the
hammer. The powder was wet.

Orlik threw himself at full length on
the raft. There was no help. He lay
still for a moment, then got on his feet,
and turning to Mary, said:

"Mary! Any other girl but thee I
would have taken by force and carried
her into the woods. I was tempted to do
it with thee, but I dared not, for I loved
thee. I was prowling alone in the woods
like a wolf; men feared me; and now I
am afraid of thee, Mary. Hast thou given
me a love powder? Thou wilt not wed
me; then welcome death. I shall save
thee or perish. If I perish think kindly
of me and pray for me, my dear one. Is
it my fault that I love thee? I never

wronged thee. Oh, Mary! Mary! fare-
well, my love, my life!"

Before she could stop him he plunged
into the water and began swimming. For
a few moments she could see in the darkness his head and arms as he breasted the
current, for he was a strong swimmer.
Soon he was lost to view. He was swimming for help to save her life. The swift
currents buffeted him and drove him back,
but he fought bravely on. If he could
only escape this current and enter a favor-
ing one, he might yet reach the boat.
Despite his superhuman efforts he made
but little headway. The thick, muddy,
yellow water splashed in his face: then
raising his head above the water and
breathing deeply, he looked for the light
of the rescuing boat. Sometimes a more
violent wave dashed him back or lifted
him on its crest; he breathed with difficulty; he felt cramps in his legs. He

thought he would fail; then something whispered into his ear, as if the beloved voice of Mary, "Save me," and again he fiercely renewed his efforts. He panted, labored, and spurted the water from his mouth, with eyes staring wildly. If he had turned back he could easily have reached the raft with the current, but he never thought of this. The light of the boat was coming nearer, for it was caught by the same current that he was now combating. Suddenly he felt that his knees and legs had become stiff. He made a few more despairing struggles. . . . The boat was near him. "Help! help!"

The last word was drowned in his throat. A wave went over his head. He appeared once more. The boat was there; he could hear the splashing of the oars and the sounds of the rowlocks; he strained his voice once more and cried for help. They heard him, and the strokes of the oars

became faster.   But Orlik sank again, a
stupendous vortex caught him.   One hand
was raised above the water, then he disappeared forever.

Meanwhile Mary sat on the raft by the
dead body of her father, staring vacantly
at the distant light.   The current was
carrying it to her.   She saw the outline of
the boat, the oars at its sides, moving in
the light like the red legs of some huge
insect.   She gave some piercing calls.

"Eh, Smith," said a voice in English,
"I could swear I heard a cry for help, and
I can hear it again."

Shortly strong arms were lifting Mary
from the raft to the boat, but Orlik was
not there.

Two months later Mary left the hospital
in Little Rock, and with the little money
given to her by some kind people she
started for New York.

But this money was not enough.   Part

of the way she was compelled to walk on foot and, having learned to speak a little English, the rest of the way she begged a ride from the conductors. Many people had pity on this poor, sick, pallid girl, with her great blue eyes, who looked more like a shadow than a human being, and whose tears excited sympathy. People did not treat her unkindly: it was life with its hard lessons.

What could she do in the American whirl with its vast interests—this wild field flower from Lipintse? How could she help herself? This Juggernaut car would crush the life out of her frail body, as the wheels of the wagon crushes the flowers in its way.

With hands trembling from weakness she pulled the bell at the door of the old gentleman's house in New York.

A strange face appeared at the door.

"Is Mr. Zlotopolski at home?"

"Who is he?"

"A noble gentleman." Then she showed his card.

"He is dead."

"He is dead? Where is his son, Mr. William?"

"He has left the city."

"And Miss Jenny?"

"She has gone away too."

The door was shut in her face. She sat on the doorstep and began to wipe her eyes. She was again in New York, alone, without help, without protection, without money, with God only to depend on.

Should she remain here? Never! She would go to the docks, embrace the feet of the ship captains and beseech them to take her, and, if they would take her across the water, she would walk on foot through Germany and return to Lipintse. John is there, and she has no one now but him in this wide world. If he will not fold her to his heart, if he has forgotten her, if he repulses her, she will then have the consolation of dying at his feet.

She went to the docks, begged and pleaded with the German captains. They would have taken her if she had been better dressed and nourished: she would then have been beautiful. They would be very glad, but—the rules forbid them—besides, it is a bad precedent—let her, then, cease her pleading.

For several nights she slept on the same pier from which her poor crazed father had attempted to drown her on that memorable night. As before she lived on the refuse cast up by the water. Fortunately it was summer and warm.

Every day she went to the German docks and begged for mercy, and every day it was in vain. She had the peasant persistency, but her strength was leaving her. She felt that if she did not sail soon, she

too would shortly die, as had all those
with whom her fate had been bound.

On a certain morning she dragged herself with a great effort, and with the
thought that perhaps this would be the
last time she could do so, for her strength
would not last till to-morrow. She had
decided to ask no more, but to steal upon
the first boat leaving for Europe and quietly stow herself away somewhere in the
hold. When they should find her on the
open sea they would not throw her into
the water; and if they did, what of it? It
was all one to her how she should die, if
die she must. At the gangway of the
steamer they closely scrutinized every pas-
senger, and on her first attempt the watch-
man rudely pushed her aside. She was
dazed, and sat down on a pile of lumber.
She felt strange, sharp, burning pains
shoot through her head. Then she began
to smile and murmured:

" I am a lady now, John, but I kept my troth with you.   Do you know me?"

Our poor girl had lost her mind.   She was insane.   Every day she came to the docks to meet her John.   They became accustomed to the sight of her and often gave her alms.   She thanked them humbly, smiling like a child.   This continued for some time.   One day she did not appear, and they saw her no more.   The next day the papers announced that a policeman had found on the end of a pier the dead body of a girl of unknown name and origin.